A Different Dimension

More Tales of Imagination

by Gary Gentile

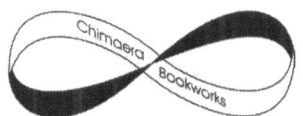

Chimaera Bookworks
P.O. Box 57137
Philadelphia, PA 19111

Additional copies of this book may be purchased from the same address by sending a check or money order in the amount of $15 U.S. for each copy (plus $3 postage per order, not per book, in the U.S. Inquire for shipping cost to foreign countries). Alternatively, copies may be purchased from the author's website, and paid by credit card:

http://www.ggentile.com

Cover art by Beth Randall

International Standard Book Numbers (ISBN)
1-883056-18-7
978-1-883056-18-6

First Edition

Printed in the U.S.A.

CONTENTS

PREFACE

In my entire writing career, I have received positive reinforcement and helpful advice from only two people. The first was my eleventh-grade English teacher, who I acknowledged in the Preface to *A Different Universe.* The second was my literary agent, Jane Butler, to whom I owe a great debt of gratitude. She accepted me as an unknown quantity based solely upon a sample of my unpublished work. She had the foresight to perceive my potential as a novelist. Not only did she enable me to break into the book publishing industry, but she provided me with the only useful information about writing style that anyone ever gave to me.

She explained the difference in third-person style between "omniscient author" and "means of perception." The omniscient author is one who switches his perception of events from character to character, from paragraph to paragraph, perhaps from sentence to sentence. In this stylistic medium, the reader knows things that are known to some characters and not to others; the reader knows things that are happening outside the protagonist's sphere of reference; and the reader often knows things that are happening *to* the protagonist before the protagonist knows. This jumping back and forth between characters on a sentence-to-sentence basis often results in a loss of verisimilitude, because the reader knows what is coming despite the ignorance of the individual characters. The reader is not *in* the story; he is above the story looking down on it.

In MOP style, the author perceives events through the eyes of only one character at a time, without loss of continuity. This integrates the reader with the character, for the reader knows only what that character sees and does - much like real life. The reader lives through the story the same as the character(s), very much like a story that is told in the first person.

A change in MOP requires a chapter break; or, at the very least, a section break. It is okay for a character to "star" in one chapter and not in another, as long as the change in the means of perception is justified by the action or by the development of the characters. I liked the theory of MOP, and adopted it thereafter.

As in *A Different Universe*, I have included the original copyright dates of the stories, because the time at which I wrote a story may provide important contextual information. The prime example in the present volume is "Let Your Fingers Do the Walking," which anticipated holograms, virtual reality, and the Internet by more than a decade. The title refers to the advertising slogan of a popular contemporary telephone company.

I have stated this before but I will state it again for emphasis. Every science fiction writer in the history of the world has been asked the age-old question: Where do you get your ideas?

Science fiction writers don't *get* ideas; they *create* them.

Most people don't grasp the meaning, and I can't say that I blame them. I don't understand how a mathematician arrives at the solution to a problem in differential calculus. To me, all those symbols look like Egyptian hieroglyphics or meaningless scribbles. But a math major solves calculus problems with apparent facility.

Creativity is the stuff of imagination. Ideas are not something that you go out to the store and buy: they are generated within by some unknown mechanism of the mind. A person with no imagination cannot comprehend the concept of creativity any more than a person who is colorblind can visualize indigo. Creativity comes naturally or not at all.

For the most part, imaginative concepts have vanished from science fiction in its modern manifestation. Today, more emphasis is placed on character development and relationships than on imagination. Not that I have anything against human foibles, but many characterizations and relationships in modern science fiction are gratuitous - tossed in for one of two reasons: because the imaginative concept is weak or ill-conceived, or because of a belief in the need to make science fiction conform to the standards of non-genre fiction, and in particular so-called "classical" literature.

I don't want to read *Hamlet in Space*, *Peyton Place on Venus*, or *Debbie Does Deneb*. There is a place in fiction for deceit, political intrigue, broken marriages, pregnancy out of wedlock, descriptive foreplay, and pornography. There is even a place in *science* fiction for these subplot devices. But I don't want to wade through two hundred pages of a protagonist's unhappy childhood, teenage crises, campus drug experimentation, corporate cutthroat activities, and extramarital relationships in order for him or her to become the leader of a colony on Mars, or before he or she drops through a black hole into an alternate universe without being torn apart by tidal stress.

In my opinion, the emphasis in imaginative fiction should be on imagination. The creative concept should be the keynote of the story and very much in the foreground. Everything else should take a back seat, or be worked into parallel story lines that help to propel the plot, motivate the characters, establish the background, or enhance the ending.

Sex for the sake of sex, character development for the sake of character development, and relationships for the sake of relationships, should be left to their Earthbound fictional counterparts where they can be read as either literature or, if the descriptive content is explicit enough, sleaze.

As the subtitle implies, the following stories are tales of imagination. The imaginative concept adds an essential plot element to each story: an element that acts as a fillip to make the reader wonder, What if?

LET YOUR FINGERS
DO THE WALKING

To Carol Bently, delicately sipping her second cup of coffee, it had so far been an ordinary morning.

She had risen with her husband at his usual hour and had seen him off to work. She had gotten the kids out of bed and had packed them off to school. And Carol, with her morning chores done, had gone back to bed.

Now, after a couple extra hours of dreamless, unworried sleep, she dragged herself out of her mental lethargy. In the dim nightlight, she stretched out one white arm past the automatic coffee maker on the nightstand and pushed a large, green button. The computer console detached itself from the ceiling and rode down a pair of hair-thin wires. This auxiliary unit, stabilized by fore-and-aft wires to prevent swinging, was connected electronically to the main house controller. It consisted of a flat screen that televised pictures in three dimensions, and - beneath the face of the screen - an input typer and a series of mode switches.

There was no "on" button, for the house controller was switched on all the time. She flipped the mode to "internal control" and with one hand typed her instructions onto the screen. After reading over the instructions, and seeing that there were no mistakes, she pushed the "execute" button. The screen went blank, but in the room things began to happen.

A hidden projector activated, and a pre-selected tape cast a faint shadow on the windowless wall opposite. The shadows drifted away and the normally blank wall began to show the tip of a rising sun. Framed by palm trees and a foreground of roses and low azalea bushes, the sun spread a glowing ember of light into the room, gradually increasing in brightness as the sun loomed larger and pealed off the horizon, reflecting off occasional waves from a tropical shore. The fragrance of flowers filled the bedroom along with the scent of early morning dew. Minutes later, as the sun rose high in the artificial sky, Carol came to full awakening, her mind unveiled like the pistil in a blossoming flower.

Armed with two cups of coffee she was now ready to face the world. She pushed a button alongside the bed; the mattress crinkled up into a sitting position. She placed the now empty cup on the nightstand as the bed converted itself into a recliner. She made a few minor adjustments until the posture suited her. Then she reached for the input typer, checking that it was still on "internal control" mode, and began her morning chores.

Carol typed a request for present house conditions. Instantly the screen was filled with facts and figures pertaining to all rooms and listing control data: temperature, humidity, air pressure, oxygen content, and so on. Then she typed the changes she wanted: increase the temperature (because there was only one body in the house instead of four); a little less humidity (she was always arguing with John about that, but with him gone she could do what she pleased); air pressure was standard; more oxygen (the sleeping body did not require as much as one that was awake). One by one, she checked off the changes that she wanted made, just as she did every day of her life. There was such a thing as a master control unit that could be installed and connected with the main house controller, but John would not agree to the expense of installation, synchronization, and maintenance. So, she had to do all the work herself.

With the menial tasks completed, she decided to tune in her favorite talk show. She switched the mode to "television" and typed a request for a daily schedule. Mentally she ran her finger down the list printed on the screen, found the program she wanted, and typed the channel into the selector.

Most of the daily programs were geared for the housewife. This particular one was a talk show that specialized in panel discussions. The topic for the day was household expediency and managing techniques. There were some interesting problems discussed, and Carol made notes by typing them into the recall mode so she could review them later. What was more interesting, however, was the commercial advertisement on redecorating. There were new fashions for furniture, the latest time-saving gadgets, and the latest wall scenes. Carol was primarily attracted by the wall scenes that depicted new and unusual designs. John did not like having the walls changed because of the labor costs. But then, he didn't have to look at the same four walls all day long, week in and week out. She made up her mind to pick out a new design and have it installed today. John would just have to understand.

Her attention was temporarily distracted by the telephone buzzer. Too late she thought about putting the receiver mode on "busy." Carol hated being interrupted when she was watching something interesting.

Anyway, it was probably only her mother. She was always calling early in the morning because she had nothing else to do. She didn't know what it was like to be a busy housewife; her children had moved out and Father had died three or four years ago. And she had never quite made the social adjustment of acquiring friends, or visiting, or traveling, so she was more or less stuck with nothing to look forward to other than reminiscence. Come to think of it, maybe Father had died five years ago. Carol couldn't quite remember.

If she had been sitting at the main house controller, she could have watched the program and talked with her mother at the same time. But here, using an auxiliary unit with only one screen, she had to make a choice. She had wanted to get a double-headed unit, but again John would not agree to spend the extra money. Carol had finally relented, but now that she needed two screens, she wished she had been more forceful in her demand. Petulantly, she put the commercial on "hold," switched the mode to "telephone," and put on her best early morning smile for the tele-viewer camera.

"Good morning, Carol," beamed her mother from the screen, her face a mask of pearly whiteness surrounded by long curls of snow-white hair. "My, you're looking fine this morning. I just thought I'd call and find out how the children are doing."

Mrs. Robinson was in her sixties but didn't look a day over forty. What with the miracle make-up they had now-a-days, no one needed to look her age, unless she was striving for a look of maturity and experience. A close inspection, however, revealed the faint lines of her face and the careworn expression that she habitually wore: a grim reminder that she had grown up in a day and age when the modern conveniences which her daughter enjoyed had not been perfected.

"Good morning, Mother. I'm in the middle of my housework, but I can talk for a couple of minutes." Probably she shouldn't have been so hostile toward her, but she did not like having her thoughts interrupted just when she was visually redecorating the living room.

"Well, I won't keep you long," cooed Mrs. Robinson, completely unflustered, "but I was wondering how Stuart was getting along in school. I know he's worried about his first field trip and I wanted to find out how he's taking it."

Stuart was the Bently's oldest child. At ten years old, he was smaller than most children his age and a little more frightened. The school psychologist thought that this might be a stumbling block, holding him back in certain areas of development. And now that he was going on his first field trip, he was extremely upset. But the psychology computer had assured her that most boys felt fear as their first field trip drew near, and that he, like all the others, would get over it. That the experience was traumatic there was no doubt. And Carol, being a mother as well as a woman, could have understood that fear if she had tried. But, being a woman, she had never had to go through that gruesome trial of field trips and external traveling.

Carol related all this to her mother, concluding, "I know it will be hard for him, but I've got so many other things on my mind that I just leave it in the school's hands. After all, they know what's best for him."

"Still, I wish there were something I could do to help him," said Mrs. Robinson, with true grandmotherly emotion. "It must be difficult for a young man to accept, especially knowing that he will have to go outside practically every day for the rest of his life. I think they start training them too young today, don't you?"

Carol's train of thought had wandered during her mother's discourse, so she missed some of what she had said. Her mind was halfway between her housework and redecorating the living room walls. Vaguely she was aware of the last sentence, and that it was intended as a direct question.

"John doesn't think they start them early enough. He says that when he was a boy, they started field trips in the ninth year, and that by the time they were Stuart's age, they were going out almost every week."

"Thankfully those times are past. Sometimes I don't know how we even managed in the old days. What with computers as unreliable as they were, you never knew when your grocery orders were going to be delivered, or if the billing was correct, or if the screen went blank in the middle of a broadcast, sometimes for minutes at a time, and you would have to sit there with nothing to do. We even had to check our own freezers and write shopping lists by hand and order from memory. We had it pretty tough when you were growing up - "

Carol cut her mother short. If she didn't put her foot down, her mother would ramble on for hours about how easy things were today. She had heard it all before and she was not interested in hearing it again.

"Mother, I really have a lot to do today. How about if you come over for dinner tonight? We can give you an hour, say, between seven and eight. Then John and I are going to the Lewis's to play bridge."

Mrs. Robinson was nonplussed, but after a moment's hesitation said, "Oh, that would be fine. But before you go, tell me, how is Sally doing with her typing?"

Sally was the other Bently child. The precocious six year old was already being taught how to operate the complicated computer controls that would become the major function of her life. The first stage was learning how to use the input typer. Then she would learn mode control and selector switching. From there her education would follow the prescribed lines of computer technology, absorbing the many and esoteric ways of the common housewife.

"She's doing fine. In fact, you can ask her about it tonight," breathed Carol. "Now, really, Mother, I must be going. I'll see you tonight."

Mrs. Robinson barely had time to flash a smile and say goodbye before Carol switched her off, her face to become but a revenant on the screen. No sooner had this been done than she switched to "television" mode, released the "hold" button, and continued to watch the long, inspiring commercial. When it was over, and Carol still had not made up her mind as to which wall sequence she liked best, she typed instructions for an instant replay, then settled down to watch the entire show right from the beginning. This time she took the precaution of typing a busy signal into her telephone answering service. This way, any incoming calls would be automatically recorded and she could read the messages at her leisure.

Carol hated to make decisions on an empty stomach. While the various designs filled the screen one after the other, she reached for the coffee maker, changed modes, and punched a request for instant soup. Moments later, it poured into her waiting cup, thick and creamy. Then, she pressed the bed controls so that she could lie back in a more comfortable position and watch the changing wall pattern at her ease.

By the time the show had run through the second

time, Carol knew exactly which wall motif she wanted to display. Even so, she still did not want to order it right away until she had some time to think it over. She was not prone to making on-the-spot decisions. It would be better to wait an hour or so.

With that off her mind for the moment, she flipped the "telephone" mode switch and found that she had had a call while she had been busy. The computer printed a photograph of the caller along with a message. She read the short note to herself, "Flower show this afternoon. Please call when available. Lisa."

If Carol didn't know Lisa McDonald better, she would have sworn it was a stranger, so different did she look. Lisa was one of those women who was always changing wigs and getting facials, even altering her personality to fit the part - a practice that Carol considered to be a waste of time, as well as money. Besides, she didn't like the idea of having her skin injected with chemicals to make the facial muscles malleable enough to be molded into the feature changes made by the plastic molds. She had always felt that Lisa was the least bit vain.

For convenience, Lisa had included her telephone number so that all Carol had to do to make the connection was to press the "execute" button. A split second later, the brightly painted face of Lisa McDonald filled the screen.

"Carol, you look simply divine today. I'm sorry I called earlier, I should have realized that you'd be watching that home decorating commercial. You've had your old pattern for over a month, haven't you?"

"Yes, and I've decided on a new one, but I haven't ordered it yet. I'll probably do it later this morning. By the way, I like your new face. Have you had it long?"

"I guess for about three days," replied Lisa, flashing her long eyebrows so that her emerald contact lenses twinkled. The huge mound of auburn hair glistened in the light, seemingly filling out her normally shallow face, but Carol thought she would have looked better with padded cheeks and brown eyes.

"You look beautiful."

"Thank you, darling. Anyway, Martha and I have decided to go out this afternoon and we were wondering if you would like to come with us? We're going to have lunch at that posh French restaurant. You know, Pierre's? Their atmosphere is so cozy, but their rates reasonable. Then we can spend the afternoon at the Annual Fall Festival Flower Show. I've heard they have a simply fantastic display this year."

Carol was not too thrilled about flowers, but she would do anything to get out of the house for a few hours. "It sounds wonderful. What time should we plan to meet?"

"I should think about oneish. Is that all right with you?"

"Yes, it will be fine. In fact, I can schedule the redecorating for this afternoon and have it done while we're out."

"Good. I'll see you at one, darling. Goodbye."

"Goodbye," said Carol as she hit the disconnect button. She switched the mode to "television" and typed a request for the afternoon schedule. She saw the flower show listed, and it was going to be held at the Holiday Inn's ballroom. She hadn't been there for ages, so now she was looking forward to going. Of course, she could stay home and watch it on television, but that was not as nice as actually being there.

Going to Pierre's would present another problem. It was a fairly exclusive place and Carol was sure that she didn't have anything decent to wear that would fit with the decor. To double-check, she switched the mode on the computer console and typed the coordinates for her clothes closet.

A long list filled the screen, numbering and describing all the apparel that she presently owned. But, like any woman, knowing was not the same as seeing. She typed a command for review, then pushed the selector button and watched idly as the dresses, pant suits, and skirt and blouse combinations flashed onto the screen. Each time she pushed the button a new item was pictured in full color. Mentally, she compared what she owned with what she expected Lisa and Martha would wear. She just couldn't afford to be outdone.

After she went through two closets in this manner, she quit. The third closet contained casual wear and would not have anything appropriate for the occasion. It looked like she was going to have to buy something new. She typed the exchange number for the Sears catalogue, typed the style and season of the kind of dress she wanted, and sat back in bed as outfit after outfit flashed on the screen in front of her.

There was nothing Carol loved more than shopping for new clothes, but she hated to do it under pressure. She enjoyed leafing through the many store catalogues just for entertainment, only seldom making purchases, much to the chagrin of the department stores' computer timekeeper. But Sears was the only one that promised one-hour delivery service. Most stores took three to four hours, sometimes half a day if they were rushed. So she would have to find something suitable from Sears. She actually preferred Macy's. It was a bit more expensive, but they had the widest and most exclusive selection. But who could afford to wait a whole day for a new dress?

After going through about a thousand patterns, she finally found one she liked. It was a simple one-piece dress with puffed sleeves and a low cut neck; it reached down to just above the ankles. The glistening lamé material held a floral design with a soft green background. Carol fell in love with it at once, typed in her size with the ordering instructions, and included her credit validation. Now she had to find a hat to match. After many minutes, she could not find anything that suited her, but finally settled on a wide-brimmed straw creation with flowers delicately painted on the brim. There was a notation that fresh flowers could be ordered for the hat any time twenty-four hours a day, and delivery was promised in less than thirty minutes. She picked out a floral arrangement that went with the green lamé dress, typed her hat size, and added ordering instructions with her personal credit code. The rest was up to the computer.

Carol pushed the computer console back against the wall. As much as she hated to do it, she simply had to get up and go to the bathroom. She wrapped her nightgown tightly around her body, threw back the covers, pushed a button alongside the bed to unseal the plastic canopy, and stepped out into the pre-warmed, oxygenated, humidified air of the bedroom. So perfectly attuned had been her earlier computer settings that from sealed bed to open room she hardly noticed the transition.

An hour later, she emerged from the bathroom completely cleaned and refreshed, but nearly naked. Her makeup was impeccably painted, her wig (the blonde one) combed in the latest fashion, her daytime teeth brushed, her skin scented. The manicure machine had done a fine job on her fingernails, but when she inserted her feet into the pedicure attachment, the motor (both devices used the same one) had begun to smoke, and about halfway through the procedure, the right foot box burned out altogether. As if she didn't already have enough to worry about, *that* had to happen - and on a day when she was going out!

Since the dress hadn't arrived yet, she sat down on the bed and pulled out the computer console. She called the maintenance department and left a message on the work schedule: she typed the problem, and ordered the time at which she wanted the repair work done. One o'clock sounded about right; she would be out then, and when she returned the problem would be fixed. After all, they were paying for maintenance protection, so they might as well use it. It cost enough.

Then she dialed the home decorating establishment that had been advertising that morning and asked to leaf through their stock of patterns. She knew which one she wanted, but did not recall the stock number and had forgotten to earmark it. A recording asked for color categories and coordination factors to help in locating the proper pattern. Carol typed what she could remember. When the different patterns and colors flashed onto the screen, she pushed the fast button, carefully scanning each one as it illuminated the screen for one second. She saw the one she wanted, halted the action, and typed out her house number and credit code in the appropriately included order blank. She also punched in the time, between one and four, so that she would not have to be there when the reconstruction crew came to do the installation. It was such a nuisance trying to get anything done with workers around. They always made so much noise, and always wanted to chat, as if she cared about their petty problems. Why couldn't they just do their work unobtrusively and leave her alone?

By the time her work was done, the dress ensemble had arrived in the collector chute. She opened the box and pulled out the freshly decorated hat. True to the supplier's word, the flowers were fresh and fragrant. The band was a little tight because of her recently coifed hair, but she could compensate for that.

Underneath the hat, neatly folded in protective plastic, was the green lamé dress. It looked even better in physical presence than it had on color television; the dotted flowers were bright and prismatic. It was sleek and sheer, made of the latest synthetics, and sparkled even in the subdued bedroom lighting. It would show perfectly in Pierre's soft atmosphere.

Carol stood in front of the mirror as she donned the dress. Naturally, it fit perfectly. Once, a couple weeks ago, she had ordered a dress and the wrong size had been delivered and she had had to wait another thirty minutes while the mistake had been corrected. But computer errors were rare nowadays. It was not like it used to be in grandmother's time.

Carol returned to the computer console by the bed and typed viewing instructions for her shoe rack. She had a wide variety of shoes, but most of the ones that went with the dress were the open-toed style; with her half completed pedicure, they would be unsuitable. She set the selector on scan and flipped through her entire stock of footwear. She went through the stock a second time, finally deciding on a pair of brown suede, closed-toe shoes with a two-inch heel. When they appeared on the screen she punched the activate button. Deep in the hidden recesses of the storage area, a mechanical arm reached out and grabbed the required box of shoes, dropped it on a conveyor belt, and seconds later delivered it to the indoor delivery receptacle, adjacent to the receiver station that still held the dress box. She slipped into the shoes, danced around in front of the mirror, scowled, but determined that they would have to do, as it was too late to find and order a new pair. She threw all the boxes into the disposal chute, fluffed up her hair under the hat, and at last was ready to leave the bedroom.

At the touch of a button, the hermetic seal was broken, the movement of the door accompanied by a slight gasp of air as the atmospheric pressures of the two rooms equalized. The heavy plastic slab that was the door popped from the suction of the rubber gasket and slid into the wall, revealing the entertaining quarters of the house. Like Dorothy peering into the Land of Oz, Carol's step into the living room was like a descent into another world.

The living room, as all the rooms in the house, had no windows. The walls were made of high reflective, lenticular, achromatic material lighted from behind by rear-screen movie projectors which, by utilizing sophisticated stereoptics, lent realistic imagery to the restless scene. The backdrop of the north wall was that of a lush jungle with canopied trees and creeping lianas. Real lianas - or rather, plastic replicas - were draped over the sofa and chairs, lending authenticity to the three dimensional panorama. Beyond the dining room table stretched a vast African veldt that occupied the other three walls. The gently undulating grassland was populated by seemingly live indigenous creatures. A herd of giraffes browsed nearby, while from the shade of a low tree, a pride of lions looked on unconcerned; in the distance a herd of elephants moved across two

walls and vanished from sight as they passed beyond
the perimeter of the dense jungle against which the living room sat, giving the impression that they were mere
actors walking off stage; overhead a monkey leaped
from tree to tree, as some of the limbs were projected
onto the ceiling.

In addition to this illusion of flowing motion, the
sound effects were activated too. Calling tropical birds
(for the moment hidden in the bushes), the screeching
of the monkeys, and the thundering hoof beats from the
receding elephants filled out the panoply of reality.
Meanwhile, the fragrance of the bedroom became the
subdued odor of musky animal flesh and raw earth,
wafted by a gentle breeze over the flowing savanna.

Carol hesitated for just a moment before stepping
over the threshold, a little frightened at the stark reality of the illusion. Sometimes, the scenes were so real
that the children were uncomfortable until they could
be reassured that they were actually safe and sound in
the comfort of their own home. But eventually one
became conscious of the walls surrounding the furniture, of the real ceiling above, of the carpeted floor
which ended abruptly, imbuing a kind of security that
placed the moving mural into the realm of a rather well
done movie - which in fact it was.

Not being in the mood for viewing, Carol walked to
the wall controls and switched off the animation, freez-
ing a flock of birds in flight, stopping a giraffe in the
middle of a chew, catching the lord of the jungle as he
yawned at his harem. The sound effects were squelched
and olfactory tubes closed. What remained was now
nothing more than a painted mural.

The highly reflective walls poured indirect lighting
into the room. The actual size and furnishings became
more apparent. The sofa and two lounge chairs, uphol-
stered in leopard skin, blended convincingly into the
jungle scene behind them. A recreation area was set off
to one side, while the other side of the room was the formal dining area. Two doorways in the adjacent wall
were the children's room and bathroom. Opposite was

the opening to the main house controller from which the operations of the entire household were regulated.

Carol crossed the room in a direct path between the bedroom door and the main house controller. Here was the computer that was the housewife's central nervous system, for without this she could not manage her house, her family, or her life. It was from here that all regulatory functions of the house were programmed, all communications received and broadcast, all external sensory data coordinated. And it was the operation of this intricate piece of electronic machinery that occupied most of her schooling from earliest childhood.

As Carol sat down in the command chair and swiveled it one hundred eighty degrees, she viewed the dazzling array of buttons, switches, levers, signal and indicator lights, overload breakers and fusible resets, and the main input typer.

First she scanned the "Christmas tree" and, seeing all green lights, knew that everything was operating normally according to her preset computer program. Disdaining to work in silence, she typed a command into the computer to provide a background of soft music. When the gentle melodies began playing, she typed a request for the day's chores. A list appeared on the main screen (there were also two auxiliary screens) in bold print. On the agenda were house cleaning, food shopping, and her semiannual medical examination.

She called the doctor's office and gave assent to his answering service that she was ready and available for examination. A formal acknowledgement appeared on her screen informing her that her request was lodged and a doctor would call shortly. She was put on standby, which always irked her, but there was nothing she could do about it. It seemed that doctors were always busy when you called.

Not to waste time, she systematically began to go through her household cleaning chores. When she activated the low level scanner, a silent beam spread across the floor throughout the entire house, showing dirt and crumbs as blips on a radar screen. The living room was a mess, as the children had insisted on eating there last night instead of sitting at the table, since they wanted to play Monopoly on the floor. She shouldn't have allowed it, as she knew how messy they were, but John said they might as well enjoy their spare time. Now, she had to clean up after them while John was blithely away at work. If men only knew what a woman had to go through to maintain an orderly house and to make a man's home a clean castle, they might show more respect for keeping it that way.

It took the scanner all of fifteen minutes to cover the floor, sonically breaking up dirt and crumbs into their component parts. Carol had to monitor the entire procedure to make certain that there was not something lying about on the floor - something that she did not want disintegrated. Only last week, Sally, ignoring admonitions to put her toys away before bedtime, had left her doll propped up next to a chair, and in the morning Carol had watched helplessly as it had been pulverized into dust particles before she could stop the controls. Sally had cried for two days but, as John had said, it would be a lesson well learned, and she was likely to be more careful with her toys in the future.

When the scanning was done and the carpet was covered with ionic dust, she activated the magnetic vibrators. These bounced the already ionized dust particles from otherwise cohesive surfaces so the house air circulation system could suck in the extra debris through the electronic cracking filters without increasing the suction on the vacuum pumps. Also, when cleaning the house, extra filters were inserted to accommodate the larger volume of dust than normally encountered during daily dusting. Suddenly a red light flashed on, then began blinking.

"Darn," cursed Carol. "Those filters shouldn't be clogged already. I just cleaned them last month."

She thumbed the abort switch and immediately all cleaning action ceased. Flipping a mode switch put her back on the circuit with the computer. She typed instructions to have the filters swung out of their frames so they could be de-ionized and turned around. When they were dropped back into position, the dust that had been adhering to the upstream side would fall off and get sucked into the cracking unit. Then, she had to start the cleaning cycle from the beginning and wait while all the air in the house was purified. The job was almost done when the call light lit and the buzzer sounded. The computer screen flashed a message to her.

The doctor was ready for the examination and requested Carol to please come to the computer console and activate the hologram receptor. Carol waited a few anxious seconds until the timing circuit on the cleaning cycle terminated - she didn't like to have to worry about in-house procedures during visitations - and typed her consent. She flipped the hologram receptor switch, then swung the typer out of the way so there was nothing between her and the full-sized computer screen.

The doctor's image suddenly appeared on the screen, standing confidently. He was dressed in the universal garb of his profession: white smock, suit pants, black shoes, and ambiguous smile.

"Good morning, Mrs. Bently. How are we feeling today?"

"Pretty good, thank you. And you?"

"Busy as usual, but I can't complain. How are John and the children - Stuart and Sally, isn't it?"

"Yes, they're all fine. I think the children will be in for their check-up soon."

"Doing well in school, I trust?"

"Yes, and enjoying it too, except for Stuart, who is a little worried about his first field trip."

"He'll get over that soon enough, don't you worry. It's something we all have to go through in our childhood. I'm sure he'll be fine." Carol nodded affirmatively. With the pleasantries out of the way, the doctor launched into his bedside manner. "Are you feeling that there is anything wrong, or is this just a periodic examination?"

"Well, for the most part I feel pretty good. But I have been having an abnormal number of headaches lately and a sort of run down feeling, especially at the end of the day."

"Ah, I see. Well, I'm sure we can clear that up with no trouble, Mrs. Bently. Please place your hands on the arm of your chair and do not move while I conduct the examination." The doctor turned to the side and stepped up to a dais-mounted computer console. Deftly he ran his fingers over the input typer and pushed several buttons and levers. The screen mounted on top of the typer printed Carol's entire medical history, complete with childhood diseases, accidents, cuts, bruises, complaints, prescriptions, and results: in fact, everything that had ever happened to her, even if it required nothing more than a bandage or an aspirin. He studied it for several seconds, then turned and faced Carol.

As she watched, the doctor walked toward her, stepped out of the screen, and in three-dimensional form stood before her!

In actuality, the doctor never left his office. His image, attuned to Carol's hologram projector, simulated his presence. As he seemed to walk around her, peering into eyes, ears, nose, and other orifices, listening to her heartbeat and taking her blood pressure, what really happened was that a miniature box of manipulative instrumentation, suspended by fine wires, circled around her. The device contained a camera (the doctor's eyes), assorted grapples and waldoes (his hands), and a wide range of medical instruments. At the same time, probes that were part of the command chair took various readings of Carol's primary functions: pulse rate, blood pressure, and respiration, in addition to taking X-rays, blood samples, and temperature. While these anatomical checks were made and tabulated on the doctor's computer screen for comprehensive analysis, he maintained a light conversational tone and discussed her psychiatric health.

"I see that you have a history of hypertension and mental unrest. The last time, I suggested that you get out more often - either traveling or visiting friends."

"I've been doing that, even though John doesn't like going out at night. He says if he spends all day outside, why should he go out at night too? I manage to get him out once in a while, but mostly I go without him. Today I'm going to the flower show with some friends, and tonight Mother is coming over for dinner. Then, John and I are going to play bridge with the Lewis's."

"Well, that's just fine. You know it doesn't pay to stay in the house all day. All work and no play are bad for your health. John should realize that too. Ah, results are beginning to arrive."

The doctor walked away from Carol and, like Alice stepping through the looking glass, stepped back into the screen. He hummed and nodded as he read facts and figures.

"Blood pressure is a little high, although it is nothing to worry about. Urinalysis shows a slight chemical imbalance. I would recommend a little less sugar in your diet. That cavity in your right premolar is getting larger, and you might want it taken care of. Next week, perhaps. Other than that, you're in fine shape."

"Oh, thank you doctor."

"I'm going to send you some pills for your blood pressure. Take them every six hours for a couple days and we'll see what that does. I have now disconnected the probe circuits in your chair, and you can return to work. Good day, Mrs. Bently."

"Good day, doctor, and thank you."

The screen went dead and the input typer swung back into position between Carol and the screen. She felt more at ease now that the examination was over. She was hardly aware of the needles and pinpricks administered by the doctor. It was good to have such a competent and courteous medical staff.

Consulting the computer chronometer, she decided that she would just about have time to do the food shopping before the children came home from school. She typed "refrigerator" into the computer, punched the memory button, and instantly the screen filled with an alphabetically arranged list of all the food items in their stores. Next to each item was the quantity remaining, and in the last column, the duration that amount was expected to last, assuming present consumption was unchanged. Items that were dangerously low and were likely to run out within the week were printed in red.

Many of the products were on the automatic delivery schedule: that is, they were common consumables consumed with such frequency that without instruction they were delivered every week, the easiest and most efficient way of handling recurring food staples. What she had to worry about mostly were foods that were consumed for dinner engagements and parties, and items that, for one reason or another, were consumed quicker than they were scheduled to last.

Meticulously, Carol scrolled down the long list of available foods, typing instructions into the computer as she found items that she wanted to restock. By typing the name of the item, the code number, and the quantity, Carol kept a separate list on an alternate memory mode.

The children must have been sneaking into the refrigerator for snacks, for she noticed that there was a definite deficiency of such comestibles as cereal, crackers, chocolate, and potato chips. For comparative purposes, she looked in the computer's memory system to see how much of those items had been eaten on a weekly basis during the past six months. There was an unusual amount of chocolate and potato chips being consumed, much more than was healthy for the children, although John was often the culprit eating snacks during late night movies. Well, she would have to put a stop to it, so she cancelled those items from automatic delivery, but increased the delivery of cereal and crackers. Then, as an afterthought, she ordered more milk for the week.

Before the shopping list was completed, Carol consulted the calendar of upcoming events, to see how many and what kind of engagements were scheduled for the week. From this she prescribed the various luncheon and dinner menus, typed what she wanted into the computer, and had it collated with the rest of her order. Now she was ready to shop.

Carol, being a conscientious housewife, was always looking for ways to save money. Unlike some of her friends (Martha Silverman, for one, who just ordered whatever she needed from whatever store happened to catch her eye, regardless of how much was charged), she believed in comparative shopping. It was a little more work, but the money saved was well worth the time spent. First, she had all the store advertisements flashed onto her screen, picking out whatever was on sale that week at that particular store and making note of it in the memory bank. King Soopers usually had the cheapest prices, but other stores specialized in certain items, and she would buy from them what they had on sale. After perusing all the advertisements and making notes of all the sales, she then returned to the King Soopers list and ordered all the other items that were not on sale, taking care to make certain that she bought in quantity whenever that made prices cheaper. When everything had been logged in the memory bank, she made a last minute check by cross-indexing her pantry list. When everything was satisfactory, she pushed the execute button, gave her credit information, and the orders were automatically placed in the stores for which she had compiled sales lists.

Delivery would normally take anywhere from four to six hours, and the items would automatically be placed in the proper storage area in the pantry, whether it be refrigerator, freezer, or dry goods. The dinners usually came pre-packed with attendant vegetables and dessert so they could be taken out of the freezer as a unit, heated, and served within minutes. That saved pushing extra buttons for special side dishes and gave the household a uniform meal. Disposable trays and silverware abolished the necessity of dishwashing.

At that moment, a sound other than the lilting background music came to Carol's ears: it was the gasp of air that accompanied the unsealing of a heavy hermetic door. She swiveled in the command chair just as the children's bedroom door opened and two, tassel-haired children exploded into the room. Oh, god, thought Carol, it must be lunchtime already.

Two tow-headed, cream-colored bundles raced across the floor and attached themselves to Carol's legs, each clamoring for attention. Carol donned her best smile and greeted them with an air of nonchalance.

"Guess what I learned in school today, Mommy," cried little Sally, showing more enthusiasm than usual. "I learned all about food supplements and vitamin deficiency. And then I saw a movie on meal selection and prep . . . prep . . . preparation," she shouted exultantly. "And they even showed me how to program the computer to get all the nutritional information about all the foods we normally eat."

"Shut up, squirt," scowled Stuart, feeling very much older and more important than his little sister. He pulled on his mother's leg to get her attention. "Mom, I got my preliminary psych exam for the field trip this morning and this afternoon they're going to take me on a make-believe trip. I won't be going for real, but it will seem like the real thing, with corridors and open space and lots of people. I don't want to go. Do I hafta?"

"You're just a scaredy cat," chided Sally.

"I am not," Stuart retaliated. "You can say that because you won't ever have to go outside like men do." Then, turning his attention to his mother, he continued, "Mom, why do they make me do what I don't want to do?"

Carol put aside her exasperation and tried to seem concerned. "Well, if no one ever went outside, how would all the work get done? Who would make all the things we need? Who would deliver our packages? Who would arrange the concerts and the operas and the flower shows?"

With that last thought in mind, Carol suddenly remembered that she had a luncheon engagement in the afternoon, followed by the flower show. If she were the least bit late, Lisa and Martha would leave without her. She decided to put an end to all discussion and get the children their lunch and back to school.

"If you have any other questions, I suggest you save them for your father, tonight."

"Oh, but Mom, I don't want to go outside. I like it here."

"I know, Stuart, but someone has to keep the city going and men are the most suited for it. After all, men are stronger and handier and a lot less afraid than women. That's why they have to go outside: to do the manly chores while the women stay at home and take care of the house."

"Does that mean that I'll never have to go outside, Mommy?" asked Sally.

"Well, you'll have to get married and take care of a house of your own someday."

"But I don't want to leave you and Daddy. I like it here."

"You're just a scaredy cat," teased Stuart, seeing his chance to get back at her.

"I am not."

"You are so."

"Children, children, that's quite enough. Please, let's get on with lunch, because I have an appointment this afternoon and I can't afford to be late. Now, what would you like to eat?"

The idea of food interrupted their trend of thought and brought in something of more immediate importance.

"I want a hamburger," said Stuart.

"Yich," mimicked Sally. "Hamburgers come from animals and they're alive and bloody. I want a salad with vitamin-enriched dressing. It's healthier and you don't have to kill it to eat it."

"That's not true," cried Stuart.

"It is so," retorted Sally.

"Children, will you please stop it. For your information, all the food we eat is synthetic, so nothing has to be killed. Chemical essences are added to simulate flavor. Besides, each person's body is different and has different chemical needs. You will learn, young lady, that when you order food for your family, you have to punch in their chemical coordinates so the food will be prepared with the proper enrichment for the person eating it. Now, both of you get seated at the table while I get lunch ready."

The children made faces at each other, but reluctantly moved toward the table in the center of the room. Stuart strutted slightly because of his technical victory.

"Can we watch the animals during lunch?" asked Stuart.

"No, I don't want you distracted. I want you to eat quickly and without any nonsense." With that final word, Carol swung her command chair back toward the massive computer console and typed the desired lunches onto the screen. "Do you want ketchup and mustard on your hamburger?"

"Yes. And fried onions too."

"And I want Thousand Island dressing on my salad."

Carol typed the condiments and was just about to punch the "execute" button when Stuart shouted that he wanted French fries. She admonished him for his last minute decisions - she hated to reorder once she had executed a meal. She also typed "milk" for Sally and "Coke" for Stuart. The milk was not derived from cows, nor was the Coke derived from cacao beans. Both liquids were distilled from the same nutrient solution - the only difference was the added flavoring.

Things happened in the pantry. Mechanical arms rushed about selecting the items that had been programmed into the computer. Conveyor belts accepted stored foodstuffs and carried them uncomplainingly to the assembly unit. There, all the food was tested for freshness, injected with nutrient additives, and brought to the proper temperature: microwaves cooked and heated, refrigerants cooled. Within moments, ready lights were flashing on the main house controller. Carol had merely to open the food receptacle, remove the trays, carry them to the table, and set them down in front of Stuart and Sally. In the back of her mind Carol knew - although she seldom thought about it - that the computer had tabulated all quantities of food removed from its stores, and erased those quantities from its "refrigerator" list, keeping an up-to-date account of the food inventory.

Carol deigned it necessary to sit with the children more for her peace of mind than for theirs. They continued to argue back and forth, occasionally addressing questions to their mother, usually to settle a debate. She tolerated this bandying as well as she could, but her thoughts were of lunch at Pierre's.

When Sally finished her salad, Carol did her best to hurry Stuart along. As soon as they finished eating, she whisked the trays off the table and deposited them in the disposal chute.

"All right, children, it's time to go back to school. And I don't want to hear another word of argument from either one of you," she added over their groans of protest.

Reluctantly they shuffled toward their bedroom door. Carol went in with them and made sure they were comfortably seated in their respective mentor units. On their heads she adjusted the synaptic stimulators that were interconnected with the computer memory and education banks through the main house controller. Back at the door, she leaned against the frame with her finger on the locking mechanism.

"I like your hat, Mommy. It smells good," cooed Sally.

"Why, thank you, Sally. Maybe you can have the flowers tonight after I'm through with them," Carol promised. Sally screamed with delight.

"Mom, do I really have to go outside?" asked Stuart, still not mollified by his mother's earlier explanation.

"Yes, but you won't have to go until you're ready for it," she said consolingly.

"But how will I knew when I'm ready for it?"

"The computer knows your subconscious limitations and will gauge your progress accordingly," Carol said. Then, after a short pause, she continued, "Now, I have a surprise for you both. Grandmom is planning to have dinner with us tonight. Won't that be nice?"

During the loud burst of hurrahs, Carol set the timer and pushed the execute button. Their squeals of delight were cut off in midstream. Now, for the next five hours they would be sealed, each in his or her own little world. While their bodies resided in their mechanized chairs, their brains would be linked to the city's central computer and would soar through vast mental interstices. Hypnotic probes would electronically stimulate their minds and teach through direct imprinting the many intricacies of life in a civilized and technologically advanced society.

After closing the door and checking the hermetic seal, Carol returned to her command chair. Consulting the computer chronometer, she saw that she was already two minutes late. Hurriedly, she typed Lisa's number.

When Lisa answered, she was wearing a different wig and an extravagant dress of lace and frills. "Why, hello, Carol. Martha is already here and the reservations are waiting. Set up your holo and we'll meet you there. The coordinates are 'Pierre's Restaurant ZPG-3.' Bye."

Carol said goodbye and switched off. She swung around in her chair and took one last look at the living room, for when she returned it would have a completely different motif. Gone would be the chirping birds, the browsing giraffes, the gray, thundering herds of elephant, the curious lions. She sighed once, then swung back to face the control panel. It was time to get ready to travel.

"Traveling" was an exercise that required stringent safeguards. Carol activated a device known as a "black hood." In actuality, it was a dense stream of electrons that sheltered the entire computer control panel like a shield, preventing any interaction between the living room and the main house controller nook. As long as it was activated, no one entering the house could see or hear or be otherwise aware of Carol sitting at her control console. Nor would she know of any activity going on in her own home. She would be free to travel without fear of interruption. Workers could enter the house to change the wall settings and projectors, repair the pedicure set, and there would be no interference either way.

The hologram was interlocked with the black hood in such a way that it could not operate unless the hood was activated. This was to prevent any interference with Carol's physical body while her mind was traveling. Interference could cause intense physiological as well as psychological aberrations. It was necessary that one's body not be disturbed while one was "traveling."

Carol programmed the hologram projector that would beam her image to Pierre's Restaurant. At the same time, she switched on the receiver so that incoming hologram images would be projected into Carol's console unit. The transceiver at the restaurant would do the rest.

She typed the coordinates that Lisa had given to her, and instantaneously found herself sitting at the luxurious and famous Pierre's. With Lisa and Martha she sat at a round oaken table amidst the dreamy atmosphere of Provincial France complete with period furnishings and trappings. In the center of the table, a flickering candle was surrounded by a bouquet of crisp roses.

The women exchanged pleasantries, complimenting each other on manners of dress, hairstyle, makeup, and anything else on which they themselves wanted to be complimented. After a few minutes of chitchat, they ordered from menus that were hung on the walls as part of the decor.

Carol, using training that had been ingrained since childhood, changed her mode of perspective. This enabled her to see her own control board while the restaurant imagery faded into the background. This was done much in the manner of a camera that was focused on nearby objects: images in the foreground were crystal clear, while images in the distance were fuzzy and indistinct. Since it was impossible to order food from the restaurant - which was merely a holographic projection - her fingers raced over her input typer as she placed her order from her main house controller.

No food was ever served at restaurants, for Carol's holographic image could not eat food - it could only make the motions of eating. The restaurant's holographic image projector was miles away from her actual body. Carol's corporeality had never left her own home. Physically, her body still sat in her command chair, so that any food she wanted had to come from her own larder. The restaurant was nothing more than a setting, a projected moving background, so to speak, and her friends were mere images. Yet one had the distinct impression that one was, in reality, sitting in a fancy French restaurant eating delicious French cuisine. Once one got used to the fairyland aspect of going out, it became quite convenient to travel to restaurants, or to exhibits, or to any part of the city, without leaving the comfort of one's own living room.

Carol selected items from the menu and typed them into her computer. For an appetizer she ordered quiche Lorraine, followed by Vichyssoise and tossed salad with French dressing. For the entree she ordered roast duck with orange sauce, asparagus tips with Hollandaise sauce, and glazed baby carrots. Her favorite dessert when dining out was chocolate mousse. Coffee could come with dessert, but with the main course she ordered a carafe of Dubonnet, despite the fact that she was having asparagus. To her chagrin, the computer flashed a red light, signaling that there was none of the cherished wine on hand. As a substitute, she ordered red Burgundy at room temperature. Like the children's lunch, it was delivered in its own tray within moments.

Altogether they had a marvelous time. The food was delicious, the entertainment quaint, the service nonexistent. Carol recognized the images of several other housewives at adjacent tables, and waved and hallooed to them. They replied in kind. It was good to see so many women out and about. Even so, there were many homebodies Carol knew who never went anywhere, who never took the time to visit, who did not have the initiative to travel, who enjoyed staying home in a state of almost virtual hibernation. Those women she felt sorry for.

Lisa was the lively one of the group. She had an outgoing personality and always kept the conversation moving. She traveled extensively, with or without her husband, and Carol wondered how she had time to take care of a house and their two children. She had strong points of view, but never entered into arguments vehemently. And even with her hang-ups about wigs and makeup, she was a fun person to be with.

Martha, on the other hand, was quiet and withdrawn, seldom entered into the gusto of the conversation, and offered little in the way of enlightenment. In fact, it was rare to see her outside her own home. She usually preferred to spend her days reading and watching television - both on the computer screen, of course. She was a romantic at heart and faced the reality of the world unwontedly. She had barely passed her housewife's course, with a score so low that she was lucky to have landed a husband at all. If she had done any poorer, she might have ended up an old maid, forced to live in a dormitory with other dropouts, and given menial tasks to justify her keep. Child bearing and raising went only to women with high grades and sufficient initiative, for the life of a housewife was complicated indeed.

When lunch was finished, the threesome prepared for the flower show. Lisa, ever ready and efficient, had the coordinates at hand and reeled them off from memory for Carol and Martha. They dissolved their images from the small table in Pierre's, and for a few moments each was back in her own home, each in her own command chair. Then each disposed of her tray, punched in the new coordinates, and appeared at the flower show. Martha, however, was a little late in arriving because she had punched in the wrong numbers and found herself in the men's gymnasium.

Flowers grew in profusion everywhere, beautifully arranged for afternoon visitors. But if one were physically to attend the flower show, one would see no people there at all. Suspended from the ceiling on thin wires was a track that traced a circuitous path in and around the many floral arrangements. Spaced ten feet apart, breadbox-sized hologram receivers moved along on geared wheels like a miniature monorail. To the women sightseers was given the illusion that they sat together on a moving gondola, as indeed their images did sit, viewing the show while in actuality their bodies never left their computer console command chairs.

Along row after row of bright red roses, yellow daffodils, and fully bloomed azaleas, the three women traveled, sharing the experience as closely as if they were really there. They could see, hear, and actually smell the scenery, as input stimuli were transmitted to their home computers. And if they got carried away in their talk and missed some of the colorful displays, who was there to care or complain, since their private tramway was sealed off from the prying eyes and gossiping noise of nearby travelers. Too, the camera moved along at one speed, and neither hurried up nor slowed down for anyone. There were no crowds, no lines, no waiting, no bumping, and no means of communicating with others.

After numerous displays of flowering plants came trays of succulents from the far corners of the Earth. Cactus as small as the hand shared space with century plants fully fifteen feet tall - many in full bloom. Miniature trees and wild ferns and sphagnum moss covered earthy scenes from the far north; lush jungle vegetation, thick and steamy, exemplified the equatorial zones.

The afternoon passed quickly and pleasantly, and when the long line of flowers and plants came to an end, and each woman said her goodbyes and made ready to cancel her hologram image, each was satisfied that she had spent a wonderful time seeing and enjoying the sights and sounds of the external worlds, and sharing the experience with good companions. And who could rightly say otherwise?

By the time Carol returned home, she saw it was almost five o'clock. Before dissolving the black hood she made a quick call to her hairdresser.

"Hi, Gladys. Carol Bently. Mother's coming over for dinner tonight and I need a new hairdo. What have you got on hand?"

"Hi, Carol. I haven't seen much of you this week. Busy?"

"I have more work than you can shake a stick at." Gladys indicated a selection of wigs that fitted Carol's usual price range, while Carol continued the small talk. "I finally had to get away from the house and the kids, so I had lunch with Lisa McDonald and Martha Silverman. We went to Pierre's, in the French quarter? Then we took in the flower show at the Holiday Inn - they had some simply marvelous arrangements. Oooh, I like that one."

"I thought you might. A lot of the girls are wearing them now. The way the hair is piled on top, it adds several inches to your height as well as elongating your face. Also, it comes in a variety of colors. I think soft brown would suit you quite well."

Carol wanted to browse a bit more before making a final decision, but she knew she still had many things to do. It seemed like the work of a housewife was never done.

"Alright, I'll take it. Can I have it before seven o'clock?"

"Sure thing. It will be there within the hour."

Carol switched off. One of the advantages of dealing with the same hairdresser was that you did not have to give all your credit information after every purchase - they kept it on file and billed the household accordingly. It saved precious seconds.

The next chore was dinner. Carol went through her Southern dishes - her mother was fond of them - to see what she could rustle up for tonight. Fried chicken was nice, but messy, and she did not enjoy yelling at the children when her mother was there. After several pages of her cookbook were flashed on the computer screen, she finally settled on ham and cabbage.

She ordered a fine Virginia baked ham in sufficient quantity for four. Cooked in a fine wine sauce and served with hot, buttered cabbage, it would be something that they hadn't had in a while. For side dishes she had candied yams, green string beans, and corn pone, an old favorite. For dessert she was offering pumpkin pie with whipped cream, coffee for the adults, and milk for the kids. As a beverage with the meal, she made iced tea and ordered lemon and sugar on the side - John didn't like lemon and Sally, because of her recent introduction to homemaking and food preparation in school, wouldn't take sugar - despite the fact that the sweetening agent was artificial.

Now she did a bit of computer cross-indexing. Rereading her list - now printed on the screen - she saw that everything had been entered properly, and sighed audibly now that the decision-making process of the dinner menu was over. First she placed the dinner on hold. It would remain in the computer's memory bank until recalled later that evening. Then, all she had to do was punch the execute button and the meal would be prepared within minutes. Pre-typing was a boon to the modern-day housewife that she simply could not live without. In order for Mother would arrive with the same dinner on her hologram display, Carol called her mother's home computer coordinates and, with a complex system of computer phasing, left orders on her computer to cook the identical meal. It was easier than talking to Mother and trying to explain why she chose what she chose, and it reduced the chance of absented-minded error on Mother's part. As an after-thought, she punched in her shopping list and ordered a bottle of Dubonnet. She hated being caught short, and besides, it was embarrassing and smacked of inefficiency.

Carol cleared the screen and called Synthia Lewis.

The line was busy but the recorder was on, so she must expect to be out for a while. Carol wanted to reconfirm their bridge appointment for tonight, so she left a message by typing her name and request into the receiver. An answering message flashed on the screen, stating flatly, "Carol, we'll be waiting for you and John at eight o'clock. Bring cheese and crackers. Love, Synthia."

Carol realized that she should have checked her own answering service before calling Synthia, but now her call was already recorded on Synthia's computer, and she would know that Carol had called without checking. It seemed that everything was going wrong today.

In a state of exasperation, Carol closed down the computer and released the black hood. As she swiveled around on her command chair, the living room leaped into view. The effect was startling, even though Carol was expecting it, and she reeled back in stark, agoraphobic horror.

The room was a desert.

Actually, it was an oasis on the edge of a vast, undulating ribbon of dunes. As Carol walked to the sofa in the middle of the room, she pirouetted daintily, taking in the whole, three-hundred-sixty-degree panoramic view. Palm trees appeared to grow on two of the walls, with real fronds draped over two of the chairs, giving that end of the room a feeling of solidarity. The third wall showed a flat, gravelly area with a stone caravansary seemingly a hundred yards away. The projectors had been set to motion, and barking dogs and shaggy goats lolled in the arid, desert heat. The hologram display on the fourth wall obscured the opening to the computer nook which Carol had just vacated. It showed a bright, yellow sun about to set behind huge Sahara sand dunes vaulting hundreds of feet into the sky. On the farthest dune, a long line of two-humped camels struggled on splayed feet through deep sand; the camels were being led by dark, stoop-shouldered Arabs. The scene was the ultimate in three-dimensional reality. It was almost *too* real. She hoped fervently that it didn't scare the children.

Carol sat on the sofa, facing the tall dunes. It had been an exhausting day and there was still more to be done. John would soon be home from work, and the kids would be home from school at six. Then she would have to entertain them, unless she could get John to do it, or unless she could get them interested in watching the camels or find a program on television. After that, she would have to serve dinner, keeping the conversation going with her mother over the din of fighting children and John's abrupt chastising overtones.

At least she had the bridge party to look forward to. She always enjoyed Synthia's company, although her husband gave her a headache. Carol sometimes wondered how Synthia put up with him and his strict financial limitations. He was always imposing restrictions on their family bank account, and he expected Synthia to run the household within a prescribed budget. This was something that Carol could not tolerate. Imagine needing a dress for an afternoon occasion and having the computer tell you that you could not have it because of insufficient funds!

Well, there was time to worry about that later. Right now, Carol wanted to take a nap until John came home. She made herself comfortable by lying on her side, hypnotized by the swirling, drifting sand and the lowering, yellow orb. The caravan was still plying its slow way across the massive dunes, and a faint but perceptible breeze played through the room, ruffling slightly through her coifed hairpiece.

The desert was pleasant, serene, and soothing to the nerves, and she was glad she had ordered it. After all, if she was going to be stuck in the house all day, she needed a change of scenery once in a while.

She certainly worked hard enough for it.

     *   *   *   *   *

John Bently savagely fingered the controls of his motorized wheelchair. As the electric motor engaged, the chair leaped forward with all the speed it could muster: enough to rock it back and to jar the drive train almost to its breaking point. Monel steel creaked and groaned as the chair sped along the nearly deserted corridor away from the walled security of his office.

John didn't normally drive this way, nor was he used to mistreating his chair by harsh use. But it had been a trying day for him and he was more eager than usual to get home. He was at least thankful that he didn't have to work tomorrow. It was strain enough having to work three days a week on alternate days, but he didn't know how some men did it if they had to work two days in a row. And John, like most men, suffered pangs of disquietude when he had to leave either his house or his office to travel through throngs of men in the corridors, bustling either to or from their place of employment.

The ones he felt sorry for were those few who had to spend their whole day traveling through the city, without the relief of a comfortable office in which to work. It took a special kind of man and a special kind of training to brave the corridors and the masses. Well, he thought, there were all kinds of men in the world, and some were naturally stronger than others. He was glad that there were men to do the menial and dangerous jobs necessary to keep the city going. But there was no way that he could ever have accepted a job in which he had to be outside all day long. It was frightening even to think of the city's highways: long and unending, open and wide, oppressive with the physical presence of humanity.

John was quite satisfied to be among the ninety-nine percent of the male population who spent their work time at their desks. He was employed by the electric company and it was his job to monitor generator start-ups, transformer switching, and impedance matching with capacitive motors when the demand for electricity got too high. He was in charge of the city's entire northeast power supply.

Of course, the city central computer did most of the work. John's job, while not exactly a sinecure, was less than demanding. But there had to be someone with intelligence and the ability to use judgment rather than cold logic. And that was where John excelled.

When the computer called for more power and automatically switched on an auxiliary generator to compensate for a peak load of electricity, John had to check and make sure that all the proper procedures were initiated, that the equipment was functioning properly, that there were no red-light indications of trouble, and that switching on a generator would not put too much of a drain on the reserves of other sections. It was his job, and an important one, after the computer automatically detected the power loss and phased in all possible energy sources and picked the most efficient way of generating the amount of electricity that was required, to acknowledge and push the "execute" button.

Today had been a particularly busy day, with a total of five "executions," as they were called in the trade. First, one generator had to be taken offline for inspection and overhaul, when it started smoking and showing signs of output stress. Then a suitable spare had to be located and activated. Toward the middle of the afternoon, when intramural travel was usually the heaviest, the computer had anticipated a large power drain and recommended two operations: the addition of an auxiliary generating station and a split transformer cross tie. John had approved both and had executed them accordingly.

But the real trouble had been when a ground fault had been detected on the main external solar panels. The problem could not be readily located, so the computer had switched to power sources from other parts of the city. It was computed so that not too much power was taken from any one section, in order that no other part of the city would be inconvenienced. This meant a complex interchange of transformer banks and generator hookups, necessitating reserve battery supply while all these procedures were being initiated. Naturally, the computer had everything worked out perfectly, so when John had pushed the execute button, all the power transfers were made smoothly and efficiently.

But the ground fault had not been cleared and there was still consternation as to what was causing the real trouble. As John's shift ended, the computer was still checking possibilities. When the trouble was eventually found, it would be up to the next shift to execute repairs. It was out of his hands now, and out of his mind. Let some one else worry about it. He wanted to go home.

The wheelchair raced unimpeded down the narrow corridor and into a waiting elevator car. John pushed the button for one of the lower levels where commuter traffic was apt to be at a minimum. The car dropped silently as it descended from the uppermost reaches of the city where John worked - since all power stations were built directly under their supply sources, the surface-mounted solar panels - to a level whose primary function was cross-city travel.

When the elevator stopped plummeting and opened its hermetic door to let John exit, he was appalled at the amount of traffic. He was on a main thoroughfare, and everywhere he looked there were other workers on their way home. The corridors were jammed with wheelchairs and he could see at least four or five in his line of vision. Even with the staggered shift protocol on which the city operated, crowds such as these were to be expected, although he had selected this particular route because it was usually less traveled than many of the other levels.

John steered his chair back into the elevator and selected another level. This time, when he disembarked from the car, there was only one other wheelchair in sight, and the driver was going the other way. This level was commonly avoided because the ceiling was too high and the corridors too wide for that comforting feeling of closeness. But to John, this was less intolerable than the presence of fellow workers.

As John scooted along the corridor, several wheelchairs emerged from an adjoining passageway. He veered around them by steering all the way to the far wall. He looked straight ahead, ignoring their presence, avoiding direct eye contact. It wasn't that he was afraid of them; it was just that they were strangers and as such represented an unknown quantity.

When they were past, he took the precaution of checking his power gauge. The battery registered three-quarters charge, which would last him the rest of the week. Once, when he had forgotten to plug in his wheelchair for several nights in a row, his battery had gone dead in the middle of the corridor - and on the way home - and he thought he would go crazy before a tow chair came to assist him. The embarrassment was nothing as compared to the abject fear of helplessness, of loneliness, of being stuck in - openness! It was almost more than he could bear, and he had stayed sick in bed for three days afterward.

Unfortunately, John's gaze lingered on the gauge a fraction of an instant too long. Not until too late did he notice an oncoming wheelchair, its occupant desperately trying to avoid a collision. John swerved a split second before the almost inevitable contact as the two wheelchairs barely brushed each other. There was a hint of plastic touching plastic as John's chair careened from the sudden change of direction. He managed to right it before it toppled over. Once he was sure he had control, he jammed on the brakes and skidded to a halt.

His hands were shaking uncontrollably and he broke out in a cold sweat. There was no reason to worry about physical damage to his wheelchair, for that was covered under his maintenance insurance. There was little to fear about getting hurt because of the low speeds at which the chairs moved. But he had almost *touched* that other man. John shuddered in disgust.

As he looked over his shoulder, he saw the other wheelchair racing away at full speed. It was apparent that the other driver was just as scared as John.

When John had fully recovered, he wheeled his chair off the main corridor and into a side passage where traffic was bound to be minimal. Also, he felt safer and more secure in the narrow confines and low light conditions. The disadvantage in traveling the more secluded passageways was the scarcity of emergency chambers - those small, one-man, hermetically-sealed closets which conveniently lined the main thorough-fares. In case of a sudden drop in atmospheric pressure or a reduction in the partial pressure of oxygen - usually due to a primary pump failure or blocked circulation ducts, but possibly as a result of a break in the integrity of the city's outer shell - it was a man's only chance of survival.

There was a ramp at the end of the passageway leading down. And below that ramp was another ramp, also leading down. John went down three more levels before veering and entering another main corridor. But at this level there was hardly any movement; it was a residential district. He continued his horizontal travel, driving along the narrow, suburban corridors until he reached his own building complex.

Here, far from the nerve center of the city and nestled in the cool depths of the earth, John Bently was able to afford to live in one of the more exclusive sub-levels. Here, he was away from the nagging fear of radiation leakage that was always present in the upper city. Here, safety was measured by the thickness of the walls and by the distance underground. Here, his home was his castle, his domain, his security.

When his own driveway corridor hove into view, John gunned the wheelchair and raced along the narrow country corridor. He was lucky in that he had a nice cubicle that was spacious but with rooms comfortably small. It was operated by one of the most advanced control systems, and it was sealed by three hermetic doors. Most cubicles had only two doors, many only one. John not only had a separately sealed bedroom, he also had been allotted an extra chamber for the children: so nice when he wanted to seal them off so he could have his privacy. And to round out his lot, he had been given a highly trained, although somewhat temperamental, wife, chosen as much for ability and function as for looks.

During the last leg of his journey, John wondered briefly about the other driveway corridors on his block. As long as he had lived here - since his marriage and his job assignment had been arranged, his income fixed, and he had been forced to leave the domicile of his parents - he had never actually met any of his neighbors. There was no reason to, for they had nothing in common with him but the proximity of their living quarters.

As he reduced speed and turned the chair into his driveway corridor, he brushed the evanescent thought from his mind. After all, he had his own life to live; they had theirs.

John pressed a remote control button under the arm of his chair, and his garage door opened automatically as he neared it. Once inside, the door closed, and he pulled into the parking stall. There was still plenty of charge left in the chair's battery, but as a matter of course, he plugged the heavy extension cord into the charging coupler. A red light bearing the words "on charge" flashed brightly. Then he stood up and walked to the front door.

As the house sensors detected his presence, the computer within quickly determined his identity. From its files, it compared height, weight, gait, and electroencephalogram, as well as his facial features. Once cleared, the door unsealed as he stepped up to the threshold. At the end of a long day at the office he once more found himself in the security of his own home.

But when John Bently stepped through the other door of the pressure hatch, he was in for a big shock.

When he had left for work that morning, the living room walls, much to his displeasure, had depicted a graphic scene of African veldt, with rolling vegetated plains and herds of giraffes and prides of lions. It had taken him quite a while to get used to the artificial open spaces, despite the fact that he was intellectually aware of the realistic boundaries of his own living room. But even though he knew exactly where the projectors took over from reality and replaced it with three-dimensional stereoptics, he still did not like the feeling of openness that it portrayed.

If he had trouble relating to that scene, at least it had trees and shrubbery as a focal point for the confinement of one's senses. But the vista that greeted him now was one of wide-open desert spaces, vast dynamic dunes, and altogether too much empty sky. It filled him with vertigo that set him reeling and retching. He leaned against the doorframe for support. It was the only reference point that he could see in the realm of infinite Sahara sand. So well matted was the furniture that he did not even see the sofa on which his wife reclined.

It had been covered with material that was flecked like sand, while a projector threw upon it the image of a scrub bush in a mosaic of green grass.

"Carol!" he screamed, still clinging to the doorframe. "Carol."

At the sound of his voice, Carol leaped up from the sofa, the back of which had been facing him, and seemed to appear from the middle of a green oasis.

"Darling, you're home," she said hesitantly, almost as if she had been caught doing something wrong. In fact, she did not like to be caught napping, for it gave the impression that she had nothing better to do. After a dread pause, she said, "It's been a rough day, and I thought I'd get some rest before tonight."

John, taking his eyes off Carol and staring around at the desert panorama, remained obstinately silent. After another pause, she tried again.

"Do you like the new wallpaper? I ordered it special today." Then, "I thought you might like a change," she lied.

John, recovering slowly, stammered, "Well, yes it's - different. It's just that I wasn't expecting it and it came as quite a surprise."

"I hope you like it, darling."

Not to be outdone, he replied, "Oh, yes. I like it. It will just take a little getting used to, that's all."

Carol delicately picked her way around the sofa and

walked close to John. She kissed him on the cheek and said, "Can I get you something to drink?"

John, now almost completely recovered, said, "Yes, I'd like a glass of iced tea. The humidifiers must not be functioning properly and the corridors are awfully hot "

While Carol went to the computer console, John seated himself on the sand-colored sofa. As he looked over the moving montage - the camel caravan was still plying its relentless way across the dunes in front of the almost disappearing sun - he shuffled his shoes and made patterns in the sand that now covered the floor. Idly, he wondered how Carol was going to keep the room clean with all that sand there, but then he didn't profess to know the ways of the housewife and her electronic gadgetry. As long as it was done, he didn't care how she did it.

"Here you are, darling. I put in some ice so it won't cool off so fast."

John nodded imperceptibly and accepted the chilled glass. If he looked closely, he could see the outlines of the walls, where the sand of the floor merged into the projected, three-dimensional film sand, and he was beginning to feel more comfortable. Sometimes, he wished that Carol would select wall coverings that were not so realistic.

Beginning to collect his thoughts, John said, "Did you say something about resting up for tonight?"

"Yes, Mother's coming for dinner, and then we're going to the Lewis's for bridge."

John nodded again, took another sip of his iced tea. He had hoped to spend a quiet evening at home to watch television or take in a movie. He certainly didn't feel like going out. However, he accepted her statement with resignation. At least he could sleep late tomorrow and spend the day unwinding.

"How did everything go in work today, darling?" asked Carol, sipping from her own glass of iced tea while making herself comfortable on the sofa next to him.

"Things were really buzzing. It seemed like every

time I thought it was going well, something else cropped up. And to top it off, we had a major power failure in one of the solar units just as I was going off duty. The computer was still checking for trouble when I left."

John wasn't finished with his story, but Carol interrupted him before he had a chance to continue. "Before I forget, would you set up the hologram projector at the dinner table? I'd like to seat Mother at the head so we can all see her."

"Carol, I just got home. Can't it wait until later? I haven't even had a chance to settle down and already you're telling me what to do."

"Well, you don't have to snap at me. I just want you to know that it has to be done."

"Why don't you move it yourself instead of waiting for me to come home? The unit is not that heavy."

"I didn't move it because I didn't have time. I've got so many other things to worry about. And while I'm thinking of it, you'd better have a talk with Stuart. He's receiving initial field trip indoctrination and they'll probably be taking him outside soon. He's been acting awful lately and taking it out on me and his sister."

John clinked the ice cubes around in his glass. "Why don't you plug him into a psychology tape tonight and see if that will help?"

"Because this is important to him and since you *are* his father, I thought you should take enough interest in your son's welfare to try to help him."

"Why do you think I pay to have the computer school for the children? I do it so I don't have to spend my time teaching them something that someone else can do better. But if you feel that strongly about it, you could talk to him yourself. After all, he's *your* son, too." The accusation in his voice closely matched that in hers.

"Because I can't do everything around this house," said Carol, rising slightly and trying to keep her voice under control. "You think it's easy being cooped up here all day long while you're outside. When you get home your work is over, but mine never stops. I've got my hands filled with shopping, cleaning house, redecorating, and all the other chores that don't get done by themselves. I've got to get the children off to school in the morning. I've got to feed them when they come home for lunch. I've got to prepare dinner and clean up afterwards, and keep Mother happy, and make plans with the Lewis's. And who do you think tucks the children into bed at night - the fairy godmother?"

Carol's sarcasm reached the peak in crescendo. All attempt at control was now gone. She rose to her feet and groaned, "Now I've got a headache. I'm going to my room to lie down. See if you can amuse the children for a while when they get home from school, if it's not asking too much."

John finally moved away from the vicinity of the front door and ventured further into the desert that was his living room. As Carol stormed out of the room, John yelled after her, "Take care of them yourself. I'm going out for a drink." But the bedroom door had already slammed shut and was sealing itself hermetically before he had finished speaking.

"At least you don't have to go outside and work all day in the open," he soliloquized.

In a huff, he threw his glass into a disposal chute and headed for the computer command chair. He plopped into it heavily and swung around to face the hologram projector. He switched on the shield and typed the coordinates for Pat's Bar, numbers that he knew by heart.

Seemingly perched on a bar stool, John leaned forward and placed his elbows on the dark, freshly cleaned mahogany counter. Morosely, he stared around at the set that the hologram projector had made for him. The back wall was decorated in richly colored stained glass. It was lined with bottles of every size and description, stacked to the ceiling on clear glass shelves. The lower shelf was filled to capacity with polished glasses.

The nearest stools were empty, but to his left and right, spaced evenly along the counter, he could see other men reflecting John's position, arms on counter, and probably his attitude. Cringing slightly, he stared at those silent, hollow, nonexistent figures - literally nonexistent, since they, too, were holograms.

"Howdy, son. Can I get you a drink?"

The bartender had appeared out of nowhere. He was old - almost ancient. His voice was squeaky with age and his eyes, while rheumy, stared at him hard. Every once in a while, he squinted as if John's image had been imperfectly reproduced and he was trying to focus his eyes. Crow's feet danced about his withered face whenever he squinted. A great shock of gray hair hung over his ears, forming loose, bouncy coils.

When John didn't answer right away, he continued, "Just type in your order and I'll see what I can do for you." Some of the creakiness had left his voice.

"I'll have a bourbon and water," said John, at the same time typing his selection into his computer. A red light flashed on and a note appeared on his screen: "Insufficient quantity of bourbon."

"Damn that woman," John cursed. "Can't she do anything right?"

"Married, are you? I used to be married myself, so I can understand how you feel," confided the barkeep. "Make another selection, say scotch and soda. I'm sure we can fix you up."

The bartender seemed to know that scotch and soda was another one of John's favorite drinks. He typed in the appropriate sequence and was rewarded with a crystal glass of clear liquid. He tasted it and nodded in satisfaction. The proportion was just the way he liked it - as it always was.

"Damn women hang around the house all day piddling their time away while you're out making the bucks." The bartender added, conspiratorially, "And then when you come home, you can't even get a decent drink."

"Yes, that's exactly how it is."

"Like I said, I've been there myself. Wouldn't go back, neither. Don't have to. Kids are all out of school, so there's no reason to support a wife. I guess I can push buttons too, and I don't need someone to do it for me and then tell me how tough it is."

This was the kind of reinforcement that John needed. It was nice to know he wasn't the only one in the world who thought that way. He felt somewhat mollified when the old geezer agreed with him. He warmed to the conversation.

"On the other hand," the bartender continued plaintively, before John could offer a rejoinder, "Sometimes you just got to have them. I mean, after all, they do take care of things, even though they get out of hand. They keep the house neat, and the kids washed and fed, and dinner on the table. They may be a lot of trouble, but they make up for it in other ways."

John was rankled at the new revelations, but the old man made a lot of sense. Sure, he was angry with Carol now, but what would it be like living without her? How would it be, coming home to an empty house, with the same old walls day in and day out, and eating TV dinners and drinking water for dinner, and doing his own shopping, and making the beds and doing the laundry. And he surely couldn't take care of the kids by himself. He needed a woman to do that.

"Can I buy you another drink, young feller?" asked the bartender.

"No . . . uh, no thanks. I think I'll go home now. It's been nice talking with you."

John switched off the hologram projector and dropped the shield. He sat in the command chair, staring at the empty screen in front of him. Somewhere in the back of his mind, he knew that his personal computer was geared to everything that went on in his house, and that a psych tape geared to his personality had been inserted when he had moved in. The trip to the bar had not been his first, nor would it be his last. The bartender, in fact, was his personal psychiatrist. The computer used his medical records to diagnose any problems he might be having, then inserted the proper tape to satisfy his needs. But to John, the man in the bar had been real, and his talk had indeed made good sense.

With his mind now at ease, he switched on the television to catch the early news. He tuned in during the middle of a broadcast, but what the newscaster said made him perk up his ears.

" . . . power losses in the northeastern section of the city. The trouble originated when one of the major solar receptor panels on the roof of the city tripped its ground fault circuit interrupter. Automatic resets failed to keep this necessary source of energy on the line and eventually auxiliary generators were switched on to compensate for the loss, which occurred during peak load in the late afternoon. Generating stations in neighboring districts "loaned" power to the affected area, causing much widespread drain on energy reserves, but total blackout was avoided in any one particular area. This only alleviated the problem temporarily, however, and did not effect permanent repairs.

"After great deliberation, it was decided that a repair crew had to be sent Outside to visually inspect the injured solar panels. Three volunteers, clad in thick pressure suits, ventured onto the barren surface of a bright, silent, but deadly world. Two of the repairmen, Philip Cooper and Donald Henchke, became nauseated and were forced to return after ten minutes. But Peter Davidson, the thirty-three-year-old maintenance engineer of Fifty-three Chancey Corridor on Level twenty-six, stayed Outside for twenty-seven minutes, refusing to return until emergency repairs had been effected.

"Davidson, who had been out the longest, suffered third degree burns of the face from the intense ultraviolet radiation which bombards the surface of our airless world every day. Once, in the past, our dense atmosphere protected the planetary surface from these deadly rays. The three men were taken to Walton Memorial Hospital for complete physical and mental examinations, and radiation cleansing. All are reported to be in fair condition despite the intense psychological pressures of having to go Outside.

"Dr. David Coffman of the Walton staff commented on the bravery of Davidson, Cooper, and Henchke. 'The average man,' Dr. Coffman was quoted as saying, 'forced to go Outside, would not have fared as well. These men represent a small minority of individuals who are especially trained to fight the traumatic psychological strains, as well as the brutal physical rigors, of the Outside. Man may once have lived comfortably on the surface of his world, but that was long ago: before the atmosphere thinned and was replaced with rare inimical gasses, before the land was contaminated with radioactive wastes, before the environment was destroyed by man's senselessness, before nature's delicate balance was disrupted by an overzealous population of thoughtless people. Man, as a race, can no longer face the Outside world that he helped to destroy. But to those few staunch individuals who perform as heroically as those men did today, we owe a great debt of gratitude. We are indebted to them and their kind, and I fervently hope that we can continue to find men of their caliber within the confines of our great city.'

"Yes, we do owe these great men a debt of gratitude, for they have gone where few dare to go, and have done what almost no others could accomplish. We can but thank them humbly for a job well done."

As the newscaster ended the story and went on to more local news, John switched off the television. For several moments he sat still, quietly ruminating the accomplishment of those three daredevils while comparing their deed to his own fear.

True, men occasionally had to go Outside the pressurized walls of the city, but it was a rare occurrence and done only under circumstances of dire necessity. Lately, however, there was talk of sending a manned expedition Outside, perhaps with the intention of establishing some kind of scientific base as a spearhead for further exploration, or for a colony. But who, thought John, would volunteer for such a loathsome and dangerous task? Where would they get men able to live in such insecurity? How could . . .

John's train of thought was suddenly derailed when the door to the children's room burst open and two screaming voices assailed his ears.

"Daddy, Daddy, guess what I learned in school today?" cried little Sally. But she didn't have a chance to elaborate before Stuart interrupted her.

"Quiet, pipsqueak. Dad, you'll never guess what I did today. I went outside, into a real corridor, and saw other people."

"Aw," started Sally, but she was quickly hushed by her father.

"How . . . how did it happen, son? I thought you were only going to have your preliminary indoctrination."

"I know, but the computer said I was ready for it, that it was better if they sort of sneaked up on you without warning and took you out sort of sudden, so you don't start thinking about it and get the jitters. So, a teacher came around this afternoon while Mom was out and took me for a walk."

John was stunned, not so much by Stuart's admonition, as by his enthusiastic attitude. "Well, how did it go?" he stammered.

"Shucks, it wasn't nothing like I thought it was going to be. I saw lots of people, I got to ride in a chair with the teacher, and we even went down a ramp to the next level. I think it was kind of fun. And the teacher said I handled it good enough to take advanced lessons."

"Oh, you're just saying that. You're still a scaredy cat."

"I am not. *You're* the scaredy cat because you don't even want to leave the house long enough to get married."

"Hey, hey, that's enough, you two," said John, still in shock from the nonchalance of his son's frank statement. "Now, both of you go sit over there on that sand dune while I get Mommy. She'll want to know all about this."

For the first time, the children noticed the new

mural. They oohed and aahed, their attention instantly captivated, and in the vicissitude of children their age, went to examine the new scenery. The sky was a golden, cloudless bowl. The sun had already set behind the tall dune, silhouetting the still driving caravan across its high ridge.

John Bently stood up solemnly, but made no move toward the bedroom. Instead, he stared at his son, pondering his youthful exuberance and utter disregard for open spaces. His mind was troubled by a glimmer of insight. Could it be that his fear of the Outside was not ingrown, not inherited, but taught? Could one accept Outside travel with such impunity? Could man, in fact, contemplate living again on the surface of the Earth?

John saw in his son a man of the future. He wondered if some day Stuart might be one of those brave and selected few to venture Outside - onto the wasteland that was the home of mankind.

He pondered the concept, however, for only a moment. Then, he shrugged his shoulders and glanced consolingly at the four walls around him, and felt the security that they provided.

Better him than me, he thought. Better him than me.

THE INTRUDERS

The life of a reporter is not very exciting.

Everyone thinks we get to travel around the world, visit foreign cities, interview famous dignitaries, enjoy special press privileges such as invitations to banquets and new movie releases, and hobnob with the personalities of stardom. Well, it just isn't so.

Oh, sure, there are some reporters you see on television or read about in the newspapers and magazines who hit the big time, but they are few and far between: about as rare as four-leaf clovers in Death Valley. They represent about one-tenth of one-tenth of one percent of all the reporters in the world. Most reporters are like me: common hacks who spend their time pounding out filler pieces on an outdated typewriter, tracing down obituary columns, doing an occasional article of local interest, and - in my case at least - wasting valuable talent.

It's a dull, structured life that pays well enough to offer security and ease of mind, but not enough for true freedom. It entices just enough to keep one interested, but not enough to make one overzealous about the job. It makes a person wish he could leave it and go on to something better, but thankful that he's at least got what he has. You're halfway between the rocks and the deep blue sea, without the opportunity to move up, without the initiative to move on. It's blasé, humdrum, and so-so, but it pays the bills. And for the most part, it offers no more excitement than the life of a grocery clerk.

Until the spaceship landed in the Badlands of South Dakota.

Some people say that South Dakota is nothing *but*

badlands, but this isn't so. I was born and raised here and I can tell you different. (Pardon my drawl.) Although only five percent of South Dakota is forested, what isn't covered by ponderosa pine and Black Hill spruce exhibits grandeur unequalled in the continental United States. The terrain is rough and rugged, interwoven with valleys and high-walled canyons. Almost the entire State drains into the Missouri River. So intricate and desolate are these river valleys and uplands that you can travel on foot - in some instances the only acceptable mode of transportation - for a whole day and end up no more than a mile from where you started.

So what finer and more inaccessible place in the country could an extraterrestrial spaceship choose to land?

The sequence of events unfolded in a rather haphazard fashion to the public, and it wasn't until several days had passed that two and two were put together and everything was ironed out. But you have the advantage of hindsight, so I will attempt to put the story down in proper chronological order.

As the reporter for the Pierre, South Dakota, *Intelligencer* (and I emphasize the word "the"), I was spending a quiet summer day in the cool of the copy room (the side away from the sun-beaten window) blithely typing out an exposé on crime in Pierre - we had had three so far this year - when my big-hearted and big-stomached boss charged through the door screaming for me. It seems he had heard from his wife's great aunt that her cousin's nephew's boy (who worked for the county) had hauled two dead park rangers to the morgue in Wanblee in the sheriff's pickup truck. The sheriff had refused to divulge any information, but the rumor that came through the devious grapevine was that there wasn't a mark on their bodies.

The boss wanted the full story for the morning paper, as it was likely to be the biggest local news since Johnny McCoy's cat got caught in a tree in front of the firehouse and wailed so loud that she sent out the engines on a three-alarmer.

Since it's a good hundred miles or more from the capital city of South Dakota to the Park, I had to skip my morning coffee break and hightail it out of there pronto so I could get back in time to have the story written for the linotypist to put it together for the midnight press run. If our readers only knew what effort went into each and every news item . . .

I loaded my briefcase, tape recorder, and camera into my old but still running station wagon - we didn't have a company car, so I was paid mileage - and lit out for the highway. In mid August, the days are hot and sultry, even without a humidity problem, and since I hadn't had time to go home to get a thermos or cooler, I made several stops along the way for cold drinks and refreshment.

Heat from the sun streamed into the car and made it an oven. The windows were wide open and constant road dust billowed into the car, leaving left a fine layer of itself on everything. The only saving grace was that since I was heading west, the sun was behind me and did not give me a headache from penetrating road glare.

I pulled into the ranger station some time right after noon, full as a tick from all I had drunk, but still ravenously hungry. As there is no food to be had in the Park, I had bought several sandwiches at the last service station. Before I plowed into my work, I took the time to plow into those sandwiches - a reporter needs his strength, especially in the field. When I had wolfed down enough food to get me through the afternoon, I swilled my mouth out with a gallon of lukewarm water, and, carrying my tape recorder and camera, went in to see the park rangers.

The office, however, was deserted.

The doors were locked, and no one appeared after my insistent banging. I pressed my face up against the plate glass window, but there was no movement inside. I cupped my eyes to block out reflection on the glass. Still there was nothing. I backed away from the window and surveyed the building, looking for some way that may have afforded me entrance.

It was then that I noticed the sign on the door, hastily written in Magic Marker on a sheet of typing paper, and taped to the inside of the glass panel. It stated: Park Closed Temporarily - Until Further Notice. I must have stood directly over the sign when I had first peered into the office.

But that was ridiculous - not that I hadn't seen the sign, but that the park was closed. I had never heard of such a thing happening before. I mean, national parks just don't close down in the middle of the tourist season.

Unless . . .

. . . unless there were two mysterious deaths and the killer was still at large. For the first time, I began to suspect that something funny, something sinister, was going on. A slight chill ran up my spine. I might, I thought, be onto something big. I mean, deaths aren't exactly uncommon in the desert, but they are usually due to accidents or natural causes such as falls, dehydration, heat stroke, or rattlesnake bites - although I would tend to exclude the latter because snakes don't bite by accident, and only by a broad interpretation can it be considered a natural cause. But these causes of death are all explainable. And they leave a mark of some kind on the body.

And they don't close a park on account of it.

I heard the coughing of an overworked engine coming around the bend in the road past the ranger station. I walked back to my station wagon and took up a position against one ailing fender that I meant to have fixed, and awaited the arrival of the outgoing vehicle.

Amid a cloud of dust, a screech of dried brakes, and a clanking of loosely attached metal parts, a World War Two surplus army jeep chugged to a halt as the driver peeled off the road so he would not become engulfed by the thick cloud of dust that followed close behind. The two occupants looked me over.

"Howdy, pardner," drawled the driver, an elderly man with a stern face offset by an easy-going smile. He was dressed in patched dungarees, a faded flannel shirt, and a wide-brimmed cowboy hat. "If you're thinkin' of takin' Route 16 through the park, you'd better think again. The rangers have closed off the road at both ends and have the park sealed tighter than a steel drum. Won't let nobody in."

He spoke pleasantly, but with an air of finality. He took one hand off the steering wheel, reached up, and pulled his hat down a little farther over his eyes. Even in the resulting shade, his blue eyes sparkled like waves crashing on a Bahamian beach.

"Why did they turn you away?" I asked in astonishment.

"Didn't turn us away," responded the driver. "We was already in there. They came in and got us. Dropped in on us this morning from a helicopter. Said they'd evacuated the park yestiday, but we was up north on a jeep trail and camped off the road. Said there was an outbreak of mountain lions and they already had some casualties among the campers. Even radioed for a ranger jeep to come an' escort us out."

"But, I didn't know there *were* mountain lions in the Badlands," I said.

"They ain't. I lived nearabouts all my life and I never seen nor heared of them, neither. Sounds pretty fishy to me."

"It's possible they migrated in from the west," said his companion. For the first time, I looked across the jeep to the tall youth sitting in the passenger seat. He was dressed like the older man, although a little less shabbily, and had the same stern features and bright blue eyes. He rested one cowboy-booted foot on the rusted metal dash. His manner was just as rugged as the older man's, but his speech was polished with a veneer of education. "Mountain lions are not uncommon in the Black Hills, and they may have been driven this way either by man's encroachment or by pressing environmental factors affecting their food sources."

"Now, son, mountain lions live in the mountains, not in the desert. If they did, they'd be called desert lions."

The boy fell silent, not from domination, I felt, but out of respect, and the certain knowledge that nothing he said could change the opinion of one who was set in his ways.

The designation "mountain lion" is somewhat of a misnomer. Depending upon where you live, *Felis concolor* may otherwise be called catamount, cougar, mountain cat, panther, puma, and a couple of dozen less common names. And that's just in English. Add the names in Spanish and the various Indian dialects, and this unjustly maligned feline is known by more than a hundred different names. By any appellation, it's not an animal to fool around with. At one time they ranged over most of the United States, from New Jersey to California. Now they were confined to the more remote and uninhabited areas of the country and throughout much of Mexico.

Changing the subject, I said, "Have you heard anything about the deaths of two park rangers?"

"No-o-o-o, cain't say as I have," replied the older man. "They was all pretty tight-lipped and real businesslike."

"Did they say how long the park would be closed?"

"Till further notice."

"Typical answer," I scowled.

I glanced past the jeep, down the road that disappeared around a striated tower of rocky upland. Beyond would be the twisted gullies of prehistoric origin, layers of sediment from an inland sea that was raised and drained by the same forces that created the Rocky Mountains. The grasslands of the prairies seemed to stop with almost unnatural abruptness, to be taken over by naked rock and convoluted fissures sculpted by wind and rain and erosion over a period of millions of years.

The father, as I assumed him to be, doffed his huge hat and banged it on the side of the jeep. Clouds of dust fell off and dropped straight to the ground in the dry, windless air.

"Would a thought that storm'd brought in some rain

with it, but we didn't see nary a drop."

"Was there a storm out there?" I asked. I was lost in thought, and replied strictly out of habit.

"Some kinda 'lectrical storm. 'Bout a hour after sunset the whole sky sparkled like the fourth of July. Tom here thinks it mighta been a aur-or-i-al-is."

"Aurora borealis," the boy enunciated.

"Yeah, aur-or-i-al-is. Whatever it was, it didn't bring no rain." He plopped his hat back on his head and wormed it down snugly over his brows. "Well, we'll be moseying along," he said. The boy remained obdurately silent. "Watch out for them mountain lions," he smiled. In one smooth motion he released the emergency brake, eased off the clutch, and chugged back onto the road and away.

"You do the same," I called after him. I raised my hand in a friendly gesture. The boy waved back expressionlessly.

As usually happened after an interview, as soon as they were gone I thought of ten more questions I should have asked. I shrugged off the feeling indifferently: they probably didn't know any more than they had already told me.

Now, the wildcat story was interesting. Cats being pushed here from the mountains to the west, to avoid encroachment of their home territory, sounded like a logical, reasonable, and professional explanation: except that it just didn't make sense.

It sounded like the kind of story concocted to fool a tourist. But to someone who had lived in South Dakota all his life, like the jeepsters, or like me, it was balderdash.

Then another startling thought struck me in the ribs: the Park Service does not have helicopters!

I had not been given many facts when I had started out on this assignment, and so far I was losing ground. I understood less now than when I had left my office in Pierre. And the one question that was foremost on my mind was: what color was the helicopter?

I walked back to my car, started it, and steered

down the road from which the jeep had come. The next logical step was to have a talk with the park rangers and get the information first hand. They might have a reason for not wanting to panic campers and backpackers, but honesty with the press was something else again. Who knows, the story about the mountain lions might be true. That in itself would make good copy. The deaths and maulings would make better headlines. It may sound morbid, but it's business.

I had yet to find out about the spaceship.

The visitor center no sooner disappeared behind me as I rounded the bend when I came up abruptly against a road barrier. It was a wooden horse hastily nailed together from scrap two-by-fours, and wore the same sign as the park office door.

Ahead, the sky was blue and unclouded, the land cracked and broken, the macadam winding along dry streambeds and around buttes. Heat shimmers rose off the blacktop toward the sky, distorting the landscape as if seen through a silky veil. In the car, the temperature continued to climb.

My shirt peeled off the seat as I got out to remove the barrier. Once I had driven past it, I went back and put it back in place. I had come this far for a story. I wasn't about to turn away now.

For a couple of miles I saw nothing but primitive terrain, bisected by an anachronistic highway. I had the impression of having crossed a time barrier separating the real world from Earth's prehistory. There were no signs of human habitation: no buildings, no houses, no roadside stands, no automobiles, and no billboards. There was just me and that great, sinuous road.

I saw the unmistakable tracks of four-wheelers leading off the blacktop into the valleys and ravines where nothing existed but rocks and open sky and untrammeled serenity. Deep-clawed tire prints stood as mute evidence of the growing number of people seeking solace in the anonymity of the desert. I longed to veer off the road to discover new paths of adventure, and to leave behind the pressure of civilization. But now was the time for work.

Several miles and many bends later, I came upon a roadblock, this one impassible. The barricade consisted of two four-wheel-drive pickup trucks planted across the road, grill to grill. The road sloped away on both sides into deep gullies that were not navigable even with an off-road rig. It was simple but effective.

Two men in ranger uniforms lounged against the vehicles, drinking something that had been poured from a thermos flask into polystyrene cups. Two rifles lay across the hoods of the trucks.

They looked up belligerently at the approach of my station wagon. I braked to a halt several yards in front of them, shut off the ignition, and got out to meet them.

Together they sauntered toward me, their once neat uniforms now dusty, sweaty, and covered with grime. They appeared to have slept in their clothes; or, perhaps they had stayed up all night sitting on the ground. One thing I was sure about: neither one was wearing clothes which fitted him.

They had left their cups of steaming liquid on one of the hoods. I noticed the heat waves rising from the thickened tops: who in his right mind would drink (presumably) coffee amidst the afternoon heat? One of the two nestled a brown Smokey-the-bear hat over his scalp; the other (hatless and crew-cut) dangled a rifle under his arm, clenching it by the trigger guard.

"Didn't you see the sign?" said the one in the hat. "The park's closed today." The man who spoke towered over me by a head (and I am no midget), and leered down at me with green, glaring eyes. He was wiry rather than skinny, and stood with both hands on his hips in an air of defiance. The sleeves of his shirt lacked a good three inches of reaching his wrists, and the legs of his pants, with the hems recently let down and not ironed, still did not reach his ankles. He was a caricature of someone who had been caught in a rainstorm in a new suit, which had then shrunk up on him. He looked comical, but I did not laugh.

"I saw it, but I didn't believe it."

"Believe it," gruffed the one with the rifle. He was shorter and more filled out than the other, but still taller than my six feet. His face could have been chiseled in stone for all the muscles that moved when he spoke. I didn't laugh at him, either.

I cleared my throat and found my voice in the dust. "But, I never heard of a park being closed before. What's it all about?"

"It's about lions," said the one in the hat. "We got some wild ones running around tearing people up and we don't want nobody hurt."

I could see that playing the dumb tourist wasn't going to get me anywhere with these guys, but I was reluctant to admit that I was a reporter. If what I suspected about these two characters was true, I would be lucky to get away unescorted. I took a different tack, deciding to pray on their sympathy and understanding

"Is there anything else you can tell me - ?"

"I can tell you to turn around and get out of here, Mister," said the hat.

"But how long - ?"

"Until further notice," said the gun.

I took the hint. Backing toward my car, I said, "Yes, I guess you're right. Sorry to have bothered you." I kept mumbling non-sequiturs until I reached the car. Then I jumped in, started and revved the engine, and pulled a quick U-turn. I left hurriedly, but I was careful not to leave a dust cloud, as I didn't want them chasing after me in anger.

Through my rear view mirror I could see that the two wolves in ranger's clothing continued to watch my retreating vehicle. They stood solid as oaks until I rounded a bend and they were cut off from view.

But I had no intentions of giving up now. I drove about a mile, then pulled over. A four-wheel-drive trail forked off the highway, heading north. It was mostly hard-packed sand and loose gravel and did not seem too formidable. I saw no deep ruts or potholes or washouts. I decided to give it a try.

As the car plowed onto the seldom used trail, I found that the surface was not as sturdy as it looked. Very shortly, the wheels began to spin and dig into the soft sand. The trail looked harder packed farther on - if I could get that far. Before I let the wheels dig four graves in the ancient sediment, I got out and let some air out of the tires. The sidewalls bulged noticeably when the pressure was down to ten pounds per square inch. I put the car into low gear and eased down on the accelerator. The wheels spun, but the increased surface area of tread on sand pulled me through.

The car climbed out of the sand pit and reached rock. The trail dropped into a gully between two cactus-covered plateaus. Half a mile in, I parked in the shade, pulled my binoculars out from where they lived in the glove compartment, and climbed onto a high knoll from which I could observe the pickup truck barricade.

I lay down on the warm ground, stretched out with my legs behind me. With my elbows braced and locked into position, I brought the ten-by-fifties up to my eyes. The two trucks zoomed up close. At first I didn't see the gruesome twosome, but a second glance proved that they were lying in the shade of the trucks. I spotted a glint of sun reflecting off one of the blued rifle barrels.

In that whole expanse of desert before me, nothing else moved.

I crawled away to a better vantage point in the shade of a boulder. Here, where I could still see my reluctant informers, I lay down to think.

The first conclusion I came to - in fact, had already come to - was that the rangers were not rangers . . . at least, not park rangers. Their actions belied their uniforms. I knew from experience that park rangers were courteous, intelligent, and soft spoken. Their object was not only to protect the public, but to inform the public. Beside the fact that the two characters were insolent, ill mannered, and unkempt, the dead give away was the rifle.

It was a military issue M-14, complete with automatic selector switch. These men were soldiers.

I had an inkling that there was more here than met the eye. I enumerated the facts. Two park rangers had been mysteriously killed. The park was apparently closed; at least, a sign had been posted to that effect - and it was surprising how many people read signs and obeyed them without question. And here were two men posing as guards, but who were no more park rangers than they were Texas Rangers.

I breathed a sigh of relief as I thought of the helicopter that had spirited the two jeepsters out of the park. *For until now, I was half afraid that the two men masquerading as rangers were in fact murderers wearing the clothes of their victims!*

Somewhere during this exercise in deduction, I became aware of a low rumbling noise, as of thunder in the distance. I perked up like an alerted prairie dog and surveyed my surroundings. The two bogus rangers were still at their posts lying in the shade of their trucks. I saw nothing in their direction, nor overhead. Finally, I spun around.

Behind me, along the road from the park entrance, a cloud of dust clung close to the horizon. Although it was several miles distant, it was plainly visible as it peeled off the ground - a brown pall against the blue sky. It would take a fleet of cars to stir up that much dust.

Standing up and peering through the binoculars, I couldn't see anything but a wobbly blur. I folded my arms down in front of my chest for support. The glasses moved up and down in time with my breathing. A long line of vehicles came into view. All were painted olive drab.

The cavalcade passed by like the Presidential review. Green station wagons waving flags from their front fenders led the parade. Then came a host of CG-5's - command jeeps - sporting canvas tops and towing field pieces. Behind them were larger, four-wheel-drive trucks that were linked to covered, flatbed trailers. Then came an endless procession of six-wheeled deuce-and-a-halfs with the side flaps rolled up. They were jammed with troops, bristling with rifles, and each dragged a long-barreled howitzer. Bringing up the rear were armored personnel carriers and tanks, rolling along on steel treads and churning up the road as well as the dust.

If this was a bunch of weekend warriors out on maneuvers, they were sure playing to win. It was the biggest concentration of military vehicles since the Battle of the Bulge.

I dropped the binoculars and let them dangle by the strap on my chest. What had started out to be a routine filler article was quickly turning into a full-length feature story . . . if, I reminded myself, I could get someone to tell me what the hell was going on.

For a long time, I watched as the entire United States Army went to avenge the deaths of two park rangers. I felt sorry for the lions.

The two pickup trucks had been pulled aside to allow the army through. Like a long, metal snake, the motorcade wound along the road, ever deeper into the heart of the Badlands. And when every car, every jeep, every truck, and every tank fell over the horizon, when the dust had settled behind them, when the two guards had again barricaded the road, it was as if they had driven into a giant gopher hole and disappeared.

Rapid-fire ideas ran through my brain like bullets through the barrel of a machine gun. But no matter what course they took, I couldn't make any sense of the matter. What would the Army possibly want with the Badlands? What would *anyone* want with the Badlands?

The next big question was: What do I do now?

About halfway through that train of heavy artillery, I had lost my confidence. Although I had been prepared to buck up to the whole park service for a story, I was somewhat intimidated by the Marines, the Army, and the National Guard. I mean, after all, we're talking about a reporter who's whole career consisted of interviewing farmers about bugs in their crops, gathering statistics on the number of household pets kept within city limits, and writing articles about Aunt Tilda's lunch recipes. Something like this was completely out of my league.

And it was for that very reason that I was able to rise to the occasion. A call to arms equivalent to a large force of invaders could not be kept under wraps. Soon the Badlands would be crawling with newsmen. This was my golden opportunity, for whatever was happening here was front-page news, and I was the man on the spot.

I was either going to sink or swim on this assignment. After all, the worst they could do was to shoot me at sunrise.

It was mid-afternoon, so I still had about five hours of daylight left. I ran back to the car and jumped in, tossing the binoculars on the seat next to me. I didn't know how far this trail went but I was going to take it for all it was worth.

I followed the gully for another two miles until I came to a fork. I turned down the left-hand trail - if it could still be called a trail - which headed west and parallel to the highway.

I ran into hard-packed clay that my two-wheel-drive station wagon could handle easily. What worried me more was ground clearance, for the trail was deeply rutted, pockmarked, and strewn with boulders. If I was not careful, I could easily puncture the gas tank, disarrange the bell housing, break an axle, or end up stranded on the chassis with the wheels in the air. I proceeded slowly, not just for safety, but so I would not stir up a telltale cloud of dust.

Once, I heard the whirring of helicopter blades. I hid the car in the shadow of a rock outcrop, but it was unnecessary as the chopper angled away from me. However, it did alert me to the fact that the park was still being patrolled from the air.

The trail twisted and twined and narrowed and worsened. In low gear, I had to crawl along at barely a mile or two per hour, otherwise the car careened violently from side to side as the wheels lunged into ruts or climbed rocks. After this, my suspension would never be the same; neither, I reflected, would the suspension of the car.

Then I came to the final stumbling block: an old streambed cut a narrow swath across the trail. It left a channel only two feet deep but with sharp-edged sides. I saw by the tire tracks that four-wheel-drive vehicles had traversed it at an oblique angle but I knew that my station wagon, with its long wheelbase and low ground clearance, could never make it. From here on I would have to walk.

From under the back seat I pulled out some old clothes kept there in the event that I had to do some repair work on the car when I was on the road. My own clothes were damp from perspiration, so it was a real pleasure to don the faded jeans and the lightweight, short-sleeve shirt. A discarded pair of hiking boots that were packed in with the spare tire rounded out my attire.

From my travel case I took out an old Nikon F, extra film, a filter pack, and a small strobe for flash fill. With the camera around my neck and the rest of the stuff filling my pockets, I was ready to hit the trail. I thought about taking water, but I had nothing to carry it in. The afternoon was waning and, I hoped, cooling, I was not overly concerned. So I filled the only container I could carry conveniently - my stomach. Then I began humping up the trail.

It had taken me an hour to drive five miles through these convoluted gullies, and I had no idea where I might be. I had never been able to see more than a couple of hundred feet in any direction, surrounded as I was by high walls and curving ravines. My first step was to climb to high ground and get my bearings.

Huffing and puffing, I topped a hundred-foot rise above the car and found myself on a wide grassy plain. It was perhaps half a mile square and at the farther corner was an elevated peak. I built a cairn on the spot where I had climbed up out of the gully, so I could relocate my car.

The arrival of helicopters made me dash for cover. They must have been flying from downwind, for I was hardly aware of them before they made their appearance. I flattened myself out as they roared overhead, skimming the ground on the level of the plateaus. There were three of them flying in formation: hueys leftover from the Vietnam conflict. I couldn't see the pilots through the bubbled windshield, but door gunners hung out from each side, fifty-caliber machine guns in hand. They flew off towards the west and, using that for a direction, I sloughed off after them.

For two hours I eased my aching muscles over hill and down dale. The Badlands was undoubtedly the most difficult hiking terrain in the country. Never in basic training had I sweated so much, ached all over, or driven myself so hard. Minor difficulties aside, the most serious problem was beginning to pray on me: thirst.

In that short a period of time, I found myself longing for water. I told myself that I wasn't delirious, nor had I any right to be, since my last drink had been only two hours before. But I was damned uncomfortable.

And it was because of that discomfort that a most fortuitous circumstance occurred.

Stumbling down a rocky incline, muscles sore and weak, I slipped completely over a loose boulder. Headlong I tumbled down a steep talus slope, bouncing and bruising over sharp rocks and causing in my wake a small but deadly rockslide.

At the bottom of the slope I hit the ground hard on one shoulder, I lay there stunned. Rocks rolled past me, but too late I looked up and saw the killer rock sliding straight for me. Battered and beaten as I was, my reaction time was too slow to save me. The big boulder eased itself down gently on my right leg, not enough to crush it, but enough to pin it down. I struggled vainly for several minutes until I came to the inevitable conclusion: I was trapped under a rock whose weight, from my position, was too much for me to lever off.

After struggling uselessly for five or ten minutes, I lay back utterly exhausted. I gasped for air until I was able to calm myself down. Then I took stock of the situation. Probing my body and extremities, I was relieved to find that there were no broken bones; indeed, I had suffered very little injury other than bumps and scrapes.

Even my right leg did not appear to be damaged. It was merely wedged under the rock which, fortunately, had straddled the leg and was resting most of its weight on surrounding rocks. It was also possible, though, that my exertions might dislodge the rocks on which the large boulder was resting, causing it to drop the rest of its mass on my leg, and crushing it.

For half an hour I lay there, thinking up ways to signal the military forces which I had taken such pains to avoid. No ideas came to mind. But at least I found that my camera, although it had sustained some cosmetic damage, was still in working order. Likewise, the strobe still operated, at least on manual mode. Then I had a sudden flash of insight! (Pardon the pun.) I could use the strobe as a signaling device after dark.

Inevitably, thoughts of food came to mind. More importantly, I had sweated out a lot of water in the heat of the afternoon, and I was seriously wondering whether I would survive the night. The sun was already dangerously low on the horizon.

Then, unbelievably, I heard a noise, faintly at first, but growing louder. It was the crunching of stones under marching feet. I couldn't see around the bend in the ravine in which I was lying, but I knew - I hoped - that they were coming my way. Leaving nothing to chance, I signaled the only way I knew how. I screamed.

And I didn't stop. I yelled everything from help to medic, as ridiculous as that may sound. They must have heard me, but although the steps grew louder, the pace did not quicken. I cursed to myself while continuing my tirade. Why didn't they hurry up, didn't they know I was hurt? And why, at the very least, didn't they answer?

I saw their shadows coming around the bend, long shadows in the waning light. I was lying on my back so that I had to tilt my chin up and peer over my head. I knew they had heard me - my editor had probably heard me - yet the plodding pace never changed.

When they came into sight, I was almost in tears. From my awkward position, and with blurry eyes, I couldn't tell if they were wearing uniforms. All I could see were three massive shapes, unhurried, unconcerned, unheeding. When my eyes cleared, I discerned something odd about them. With great difficulty, and still yelling "over here, over here," I twisted my body around so I could see them right side up.

"Oh, my God," I muttered. Then I was silent. I think I had swallowed my tongue.

The creatures coming toward me were not men. Nor were they mountain lions - or any kind of animal or anything else of this Earth.

They were tall, at least eight feet, but slender like boa constrictors. Each body, if it could be called that, was a basketball about three feet above the ground, and it was supported by four, stalklike legs that terminated in a multitude of extensions that looked like tree roots. From the middle of the basketball, shooting out the top, stood the snakelike body. About half way to the "head," four arms sprouted, each in a different direction of the compass and in alignment with the legs. They terminated in fairly human-looking hands: that is, each hand consisted of a flattened ball or fist from which a dozen or so whiplike fingers extended. The head was a soccer ball with four tentacles, each of which ended in an eyeball, also in alignment with the hands and legs. The creatures could apparently look in four directions at the same time, but right now three of the eyes were bent around so that they faced me.

A blue jewel glowed atop each head. I stared back at those nine eyes (the others were looking over their "shoulders") and I wanted to die - or at least to pass out mercifully. But nothing of the kind occurred.

I heard a bubbling sound and assumed that the creatures were communicating. The creature in the lead lifted up an impossibly long arm and pointed at me. There was an instrument in its hand. I gripped the rocks around me as I expected to be blasted away any second. Nothing happened: no sound, no light, nothing.

There was more bubbling. When it stopped, the creatures moved closer. If I ever came near to fainting in my life, it was then. I felt a vibration in my throat and I realized that I was - growling. I prayed that my death would be quick. I closed my eyes and waited for the end.

I felt a great pressure release itself from my body. I was swooning, and I thought that this was what it must feel like when the soul leaves the body. I had a sensation of weightlessness, of rising into the sky. I opened my eyes and half expected to be looking down at my discarded corpse.

Instead, I found that I was sitting upright, leaning against the very rock that had recently pinned down my leg. The leg was numb, but as circulation increased and blood flowed into the waiting veins, tickling needles began to stab me below the knee.

I thought I must have dreamt the whole affair, but as I looked up, the three creatures stood around me in a semicircle. They bubbled at each other again, then one of them (one without the mysterious instrument) took a container off its shoulder - can it be called that? - where it hung by a clear strap, and handed it to me. When I stared at it, cringing away, the creature laid the container at my feet. Still I didn't touch it, but withdrew my legs until I was sitting on them.

There was some more bubbling, then the creatures moved away down the ravine. They didn't turn, they just selected a new direction, switched their eyestalks around, and plodded on. When they came to the rock wall, they again changed direction by sidling sidewise from the way they had been going before. They did that as long as I watched, zigzagging down the ravine, seemingly ricocheting from wall to wall like slow-motion billiard balls.

But always one eye of each stared back at me.

The crunching sound of their "feet" had long since

faded to nothing before I found the courage to move. I hoisted myself to my feet, limping around on my injured leg, not because it hurt but because it was asleep. Worse yet, both pant legs were soaked clear down to the knees. I didn't think I had it in me, but I had to go some more. I found a convenient rock and watered it profusely.

With the passing of urine there was also a passing of tension - a passing of fear. While I was collecting my wits, I sat down to rub dirt on my pants to soak up the moisture and dilute the odor.

I'm no Sherlock Holmes, but it didn't take much deductive reasoning to figure out that the creatures were aliens, and that the lights that had caused last night's so-called aurora was a real, honest-to-god flying saucer. I had to say it over to myself because until now I had been an unbeliever. Well, maybe I believed in the possibility, but not in the actuality. However, I had the kind of mind that immediately accepted reality once it was shown to me.

It was then that I remembered the container proffered to me by one of the aliens. Gingerly, I picked it up and studied it from all sides. It looked and felt like plastic but pinged like metal. It was cylindrical, about eight inches high and four inches in diameter, with a flat top and bottom. A hairline crack at one end told me which end was the top, and when I pulled it, the top came off with a plop, splashing ice-cold liquid on my hand.

I reacted violently, almost dropping the flask. Holding it away from me, I poured some of the liquid on the ground. Then I got down and smelled it. It was odorless. My hand appeared to be all right, so I sniffed from the container. My guess was that it was simply water.

If anyone would hypothesize that situation for me, and asked me what I would do under those circumstances, I would answer without hesitation that I would pour the possibly poisonous liquid on the ground. Only someone who has ever been in the desert in hundred degree temperatures for several hours and sweated voluminously could understand my actions.

I drank.

And I was thankful that they had found me, not just because they had released me from the rock, or even because they had exhibited "humanitarian" kindness in offering me water, but because I - *I* - had been singled out from the masses to participate in the first alien encounter, a distinction that was not just the thrill of a lifetime, but the story of the century.

Suddenly I realized the opportunity at my fingertips. This was the biggest front-page news scoop since Moses parted the Red Sea. I could see the headlines now: Benevolent Creatures From Another Star Land In Badlands, South Dakota, followed by a personal interview by veteran reporter Paul Whitmore. I could become famous overnight.

The thought was no more out of my mind than I threw the flask over my shoulder by its synthetic strap and, hugging it and the camera so they would not swing around and bang together, raced after the four-legged aliens.

I jogged along at first, thinking that I might catch up with them momentarily, but they had a longer lead than I realized. Soon winded, I had to reduce my pace to a fast walk.

The oddly-shaped alien "feet" left a kind of puncture mark trail in the gravel that was easy to follow - as if a grove of mobile trees had stampeded on slender pedal extremities. The ravine changed direction interminably so that sometimes it was heading east, sometimes west. But the trend was north.

I hadn't been paying much attention to time, but when the sun dipped below the horizon and sent its last weak rays over the hills, I knew that darkness was imminent. In the clear, unpolluted air of South Dakota, night came like a quickly dropped curtain. Even as darkness pervaded, the distended yellow ball of the moon peered down on the countryside.

Without warning, the ravine widened into a huge, dry watershed. A large, boulder-strewn field lay in front of me, fully half a mile across. It was ringed with mountains hundreds of feet high. At the base of one of these tall cliffs, unearthly and majestic - and emanating a bluish, pulsating glow - squatted the alien spaceship.

As I watched in awe, I heard a dull thud that sounded like a rubber mallet striking a fifty-five-gallon drum. I listened intently but there was no additional sound: the eerie silence was almost palpable. Other than the rhythmic waxing and waning of the blue glow from the spaceship, a preternatural calm seemed to have invaded the desert.

An explosion of bright, white incandescence spread out high in the air over the slumbering valley, illuminating violently every niche and corner. As I winced from the glare, in less time than it takes the heart to convulse from one beat to the next, the seclusion and serenity of the desert park was rudely offended by the deafening roar of - gunfire!

The wild cacophony of sound that followed, the cannonading and detonations that seemed to last an eternity, spanned in objective time less than a minute.

More flares arched into the sky, uselessly illuminating an already intrinsically-lit spaceship. Small arms fire, tracer bullets streaming, poured unmercifully into that unsuspecting ship. The pounding of mortars and heavy artillery sounded like dull hammering in the distance. As if this were not indignity enough, a flock of helicopters soared in from above, directing bullets and launching rockets into the melee.

The ground shook beneath my feet, the very air quivered, as the concussion of that mighty onslaught filled my senses. And through it all, humming quietly to itself, the unharmed spaceship absorbed the punishment.

I saw no form of retaliation: there was no return fire, no laser beams or blaster bolts, no planet busters. But almost immediately things started happening. First, the helicopter that was leading the air assault, mini-guns booming, burst into flames and exploded into millions of unrecognizable fragments.

I hardly had time to feel remorse over the hapless

crew when the two choppers following it met with the identical fate. At the same time, I heard more explosions in the surrounding rocks, where I had previously seen the muzzle flashes of field pieces. Whenever there was one of these explosions, no more muzzle flashes came from that point.

Even though I detected no alien offensive, the army ground forces were receiving retribution with unimpeded forcefulness and deadly accuracy and effect.

Three more helicopters hove into view in a short V formation, firing with hostile intent. As before, the lead chopper disintegrated into its component parts, sending shrapnel high into the air and far into the line of attacking soldiers, dealing death to the ground troops.

The other two choppers, flying side by side, crashed through the blazing inferno of fire and debris. Ceasing fire, one veered off to the side and, miraculously, escaped. The other, continuing to pour lead and rockets into the spaceship, had attacked too low. It caught a blade on the nearby cliff face, sheered off sparks and metal, wobbled drunkenly for two long seconds, then crashed in a ball of orange light and billowing smoke. It skidded for several hundred feet before coming to rest against a rocky hillock. As it smoked and smoldered, but did not explode, I saw ground troops scrambling for protection away from the hillock where they had been hiding.

As if that was a signal, all noise of incoming artillery ceased. For a few seconds, the sporadic sound of machine gun and rifle fire reverberated dimly, sounding now like pop guns after the roar of cannon shells. Then that too stopped.

The valley was inundated in silence. The flares either hit the earth or faded out in the sky. Where the helicopter had struck the ground, a ball of yellow flame was slowly subsiding, and in the returning darkness, the fluctuating iridescence of the spaceship still beat its silent cadence.

I breathed, I think, for the first time since the onslaught of that terrible cataclysm. My muscles were tense and aching. I was drenched in sweat. My heart pounded against my chest. In the aftermath of destruction I stood rooted to the spot.

How long I stood there, or what I intended doing, I don't know. But before I had gained the will or the inclination to move, the place where I was standing became the focal point of a retreating army.

I ran and cowered behind a large rock, assailed by the roar of diesels. A deuce-and-a-half rumbled by half-filled with troops and towing the remains of a cannon hitch. Safety chains dangled uselessly and the tow bar ended in a stump that was still molten and sizzling. The rear wheels of the truck thumped in misalignment, the tailgate was half gone, and the canvas and supporting struts had been blown away. The wails and moans of the wounded begged for mercy, chanted in pain.

A decimated infantry outfit, running at a dogtrot, chased after the deuce-and-a-half. They were torn and haggard, as if they had experienced a lifetime of horror in that one-minute battle.

Then came shouts and screams from the boulder-strewn field. A mad rush of soldiers came running and tripping as if all the hounds of hell were after them. A jeep skidded around a rock, rose up on two wheels, hung momentarily in the air, then settled down on all fours and, with gears clanking, sped right toward me.

Despite the fact that I was well protected, I ducked. The jeep banged into the rock, careened sideways for a moment, then regained its balance and kept on going. As I poked my head up over the rock, machine gun fire commenced in the direction of the still-glowing spaceship. Grenades boomed ominously.

The battle seemed to have resumed on a smaller scale, and it was getting closer to my sanctuary. The retreat became a rout as stampeding troops, some weaponless, ran for the hills. Two more deuce-and-a-halfs chugged up out of the valley, followed by a jeep. The trucks flashed by, but the jeep went into a sharp turn and pulled up behind my rock, not three feet from where I stood.

Both driver and passenger jumped out and crouched next to me, peering down the trail from which soldiers were still running. The one on my left was a first sergeant, tall and grim. His shirt was torn in the front, and blood seeped out in a rosy stain.

The one on my right jumped out into the open, shouting and waving an M-14 over his head. "This way, men, this way. Get the lead out."

The burly man stood limned in the moonlight, his face a chiseled mask. He was girdled with bandoleers of ammunition, and four hand grenades decorated his chest like olive-drab boutonnieres. His steel pot was cocked jauntily to one side like John Wayne in *Sands of Iwo Jima.* His voice boomed out with authority. He was a major general.

Now a phosphorescent glow, like the blue light of the spaceship, was moving up the trail. It, too, pulsed rhythmically. A quick glance over my shoulder assured me that the spaceship was still sitting quietly under its cliff.

Nonetheless, somewhere beyond the rocks, the coruscating blue light moved. In front of it lumbered a retreating tank, treads clawing loose gravel. It was racing in reverse, desperately backing away from whatever was causing the blue glow.

The tank crashed into a rock wall and moved no farther, although for one crazy moment it tried to climb the sheer face. When it settled down, the lid snapped open, and three men leaped out. As they did, the cause of that blue light came around the boulders and flooded the scene with its eerie glow.

Six aliens, each with a shining blue jewel atop its "head," moved in a line.

The first man out of the tank had just jumped to the top of the treads when he saw the weird spectacle. Lifting his rifle and firing from the hip, he let loose a short burst of automatic fire. Tracers flew into the ranks of the aliens, but they seemed undaunted. Not so the soldier, for his rifle suddenly glowed a cherry red and, before the man could drop it, he tumbled off the tread and crashed to the ground, inert.

The other two, unaware of his fall, leaped right behind him. One landed sideways in his haste, fell to one knee, and pitched forward on his face but continued to roll. The other landed on his feet and was running when he hit the ground. As he ran, he aimed his rifle at the creatures and sprayed the gully from side to side. Bullets sparked and ricocheted off rocks, but the aliens walked on unperturbed. The soldier slumped over his reddening weapon and lay almost delicately on the ground.

Another man started to climb from the lid of the tank, but when he saw the proximity of the aliens, he screamed and ducked back into the security of the steel cabin.

The lone soldier still alive on the ground had dropped his rifle in the fall. He must have sprained or broken an ankle, for he sat facing the aliens, while crawling backward, pushing with his one good leg and both hands. He screamed in terror.

The scene was like a surrealistic painting, bathed in blue light emitted by the alien jewels. The ensuing drama unfolded in slow motion as I watched three areas of movement: the soldier screaming and squirming toward us, the aliens zigzagging unconcernedly in front of the tank, and the turret of that tank cranking around as its barrel lowered and aligned itself on the creatures.

I stood there shuddering in fear between the first sergeant and the major general, who had realigned himself against the rock after the last of the troops had passed by. And from there, I witnessed the greatest act of heroism I could ever hope to see. The general thrust his rifle into my arms, raced out into the open, thrust his hands under the armpits of the soldier, and dragged him to the safety of the rock. And I thought they did that only in the movies!

No sooner was he back than the man in the tank fired a shell at the aliens just as they were entering the ravine from which I had emerged an eternity ago. At that range he could not have missed, but no explosion occurred. Rather, the barrel of the tank turned suddenly cherry red and sagged like a limp noodle. In seconds, the whole tank dripped and melted like a plastic toy left in the sun.

Heat waves radiated to where we were crouched behind the rock; it was hotter than noon on the Sahara Desert. The heat in the tank set off the remaining explosives and ignited the fuel tanks so that it was split open by the expanding gases.

The tank continued to burn for several minutes. The aliens had disappeared up the ravine and their blue glow went with them. Slowly the fire died out, and a queer kind of darkness came on. The moon, unbelievably, was hardly any higher than when I had first noticed it, but its yellow paleness was now a dull white.

The spaceship still glowed peacefully against the cliff, shimmering lightly.

"Whitmore!" someone screamed. I almost jumped out of my skin. I turned to stare at the general. He glared at me fiercely, deep lines of thought knitting his brow, and weather-worn crow's-feet straddling his eyes.

"Colonel Wordsworth," I said in astonishment. Then added, "Sir."

"It's General Wordsworth, in case you've forgotten how to read military insignia."

"Yes, sir. I'm sorry, sir. It's just that - "

"It's just that after five years you're still as dunderheaded as you were under my command." The colonel - that is, the general - paused to sniff the air. "Have you been playing around with some prairie dogs or did something scare the piss out of you?"

"Well, sir, you see, I had an accident . . . "

"You're damned right you did - it was when you were born. Kirk, help me with this man. And *you* get in that jeep."

The first sergeant pushed me out of the way and grabbed the still-sobbing soldier. Together they placed him in the back seat. General Wordsworth ordered me to get in alongside him. They climbed into the front, the sergeant behind the wheel, and off we went after what was left of the routed army.

General Wordsworth had been a colonel when I had been in his outfit. During the "conflict," he had served two tours in 'Nam, so the peacetime assignment at Fort Worth just didn't suit him. Neither, as his company orderly, did I. I just wanted to ease through my two-year enlistment, whoring it around whenever possible. He still wanted to fight.

We bounced along in the jeep for fifteen minutes before descending into a deep, wide gully. Shaded lights faintly illuminated tents and trucks and cannons. Sorely disheveled soldiers milled about aimlessly in the aftermath of shock. The sergeant pulled up before a tent with an American flag drooping from its center post.

"Kirk, take this man to the medical tent and then find Cardiff and Samson. *You,*" stabbing a finger in my direction, "Come with me."

The sergeant left with the soldier and I followed docilely behind the general. He threw back the tent flap and stepped aside while I went in. There was nothing inside but a long table surrounded by packing crates used for seats. A gas lantern was the table's sole appurtenance. The general turned up the flame.

"Sit down, Mister." His tone was gruff and intended to intimidate. Naturally I was cowed at first, but I quickly recognized two very important facts: as I was no longer in the military service, I was not bound by his jurisdiction; and if I needed facts for my story, this was the man to give them to me. Getting Wordsworth to recognize those two facts, however, was another problem.

"All right, Whitmore, you can start by telling me what you're doing here and how you got here. This area is supposed to be patrolled to keep riffraff like you out. Now what gives?"

I rationalized that the truth could only get me into more trouble than I was already in, so I did the next best thing. I lied like a politician.

"Well, it's like this, General. After all those maneuvers we went on, down in Texas, and all those war games we used to play, I sort of got used to the outdoors. When I became a civilian - "

"When were you ever a soldier?"

" - I missed all those great hikes, so I took up backpacking. I've been roaming around the Badlands for a couple of days, minding my own business, when all of a sudden - "

"Cut the crap. We've had aerial reconnaissance patrols out all day. If you hadn't been trying to hide, they would have spotted you."

"General, that's pretty big country out there - "

"Not so big that you could be the only person not aware that the park has been evacuated."

"It's obviously big enough that you didn't know the whereabouts of those - those - creatures that I was following down that ravine."

"There are aliens crawling all over this country but they are specifically taking evasive action. And don't try to make me believe that you had the balls to trail those bloodthirsty animals."

"Bloodthirsty? Are we talking about the same creatures? The ones I saw were kind, benevolent, and intelligent."

"Yeah, and thrifty, brave, clean, and reverent like all good Boy Scouts. Didn't you see them blow away half my army like they were ants to be swept aside? You'd better wise up to some facts, son. We've been invaded. These beasts are here to conquer the Earth and sweep mankind off the map."

"General, they were *attacked*. If they fought back, it was only in self-defense. As a matter of fact, I didn't see any return fire. That spaceship just sat there and took it all in."

"So maybe they shoot invisible rays while they sit behind their atomic shields."

No matter what he said, I could not accept the general's pessimism. My first impression of the aliens, while horrifying, was lasting and undeniably innocent.

"I'm telling you these aliens are benign."

"Yeah, like a benign brain tumor. It may not be cancerous, but unless you remove it, it'll kill you just the same."

"You don't know what you're talking about. Listen, I've had some firsthand experience with them." I related the incident that had taken place up the ravine, mentioning that they had given me water without elucidating upon the fact that I was now in possession of an alien canteen. (I deliberately slipped the flask behind my arm.) After all, as a souvenir it was a priceless artifact.

"Doesn't mean a thing," General Wordsworth snorted when I concluded my testimony. "Attila the Hun spared those he conquered but that didn't make him a Good Samaritan. Any civilized nation shows mercy to injured soldiers and prisoners of war."

"Truly civilized people have no need of war. What could these aliens hope to gain by subjugating what to them must be no more than a bunch of savages? Their technology has to be so far in advance of ours that we couldn't possibly have anything worthwhile to offer them."

"Maybe they want our land, or our natural resources, or our women. Hell, maybe they even want us for food. It's senseless to try to rationalize aggressive violence. Greed, hunger, and the thirst for power are motivations unto themselves. Once you recognize this simple fact, you must be prepared to defend yourself and your territory against invaders - preferably before they invade you."

"But you have no proof that they are invading."

"They landed without herald or diplomatic introduction. In my book that constitutes invasion."

"Captain Cook landed on the Hawaiian Islands on a matter of geographic discovery - it did not constitute invasion. But he was beaten to death brutally by the natives because they forgot to ask him why he was there. For god's sake, learn something from our own unhappy history and don't jump to conclusions."

"And you stop being a fool. Not since the War of 1812 have we allowed enemy forces to enter the continental United States, and we are not about to allow it now. This attack must be repelled at all costs by every means at our disposal."

"I think your military training has shortened your periphery of territoriality and thwarted your views on what constitutes invasion and aggressive action. What makes you so sure that these aliens are bent on invasion?"

"The first thing they did was to shoot down a communications satellite when they entered Earth's orbit. Then they disintegrated five fighter interceptors that had been sent out on alert because the UFO was setting off DEW line alarms. One plane managed to report back to base only because a weapons malfunction forced him to break formation before he got into range.

"When it became obvious that our country was under attack, two land-based missile emplacements responded with atomic warheads. Not one of the missiles achieved detonation, but both secret launching sites were utterly destroyed."

"Wait a minute. I haven't heard about any atomic explosions. And you certainly couldn't keep anything like that a secret."

"Who said anything about an explosion? Both missile bases were melted, along with the personnel inside them. The only thing left afterwards was a misshapen puddle which later resolidified into one amorphous mass.

"After that the saucer dropped off the radar screens. But the aliens weren't very smart. We figured out their trajectory, computed a probable landing point, and sure enough, there they were. We evacuated and threw a cordon around the park, but not before the park rangers investigated unusual lights in the sky, which they thought was a meteorite fall. Two of them were killed."

So the ranger tale, at least, was true. "What happened to them?"

"The story I got was that they fired flare guns into a group of aliens emerging from the saucer. Reprisal was instantaneous. Both guns were melted, even though the rangers who had fired them were hiding behind rocks. The two rangers died immediately from unknown causes."

"It still sounds like the aliens fired only in self-defense."

"Against a flare gun?"

"How were they to know that it wasn't a deadly weapon? And besides, a flare in the chest can kill just as quickly as a bullet."

"It makes no difference. So far they're batting a thousand, with no casualties. They have a weapon that fires around rocks as well as searching out and hitting missile bases a thousand miles away. And anyway, just whose side are you on?"

On one hand, I'm glad I didn't have the opportunity to answer that question. On the other hand, the consequences of what prevented me from answering were worse.

Two rough-looking Green Berets stepped into the dim light of the tent. I gasped in silent recognition as they announced themselves as Cardiff and Samson. I wanted to crawl under the table, but the most convention would allow me to do was to turn my face down and shade it with my hand.

"Everything's ready, General Wordsworth," said the taller of the two. "All we need are these last few cases."

"The trucks are revved up and the men are chomping at the bit," said the other.

"Good. Let's get going. Whitmore, I'm afraid we've got work to do. You'll have to stay here until I get back. Whitmore? *Whitmore?*" I tried to nod without looking up, but it was no use.

"*You,*" said the gun.

"*You,*" said the hat.

"Hi, fellows," I said with resignation. "I'll bet you never thought you'd see me again."

"You know this man?" asked General Wordsworth, pointing a thumb at me.

"Yeah, we know him, all right," said the gun.

"He crashed the roadblock this afternoon," said the hat.

"We turned him back at Check Point One and told him to get out, but it looks like he didn't take our advice," said one of them - I don't know which one. They were a curious juxtaposition.

"*So*," screamed the general, his eyes squinting into tiny beads. I could see the italics in the single syllable. "Up to your old tricks again, eh? Backpacking, my ass. I don't know what your game is, but you'll find yourself before a board of Courts Martial before this is over. "

"May I remind you, sir, that I am not government property?" I reasoned. "I am a civilian with full constitutional rights and legal recourse to action."

"How would you like to be shot at dawn as a spy?" The general was obviously not seeing reason. "Cardiff, Samson, lock this troublemaker up until we get back."

"With pleasure," said one.

"You bet," said the other.

"I'll deal with you later," added the general. They grabbed me before I had a chance to move, and lifted me bodily into the air. My flailing feet kicked over the heavy packing crate on which I had been sitting. It fell over, popping off the lid, and a bunch of foot-long red sticks that looked like road flares rolled across the dirt floor. I had been sitting on a fifty-pound case of dynamite!

"Unhand me, you villains," I yelled, emulating a cartoon character. What the hell, they weren't going to let go of me no matter what I said. "General Wordsworth, as a citizen of the United States of America, I cannot be handled in this manner."

That I *could* be handled this way was all too apparent. My premise was that I *shouldn't*. Cardiff and Samson dragged me toward the doorway. I tried a different tack.

"General Wordsworth, I'll have you know that you are mishandling a member in good standing of the Associated Press," (which was a bit of an exaggeration), "and any mistreatment will be dealt with accordingly."

I had just thrown another shovel full of dirt out of my grave.

"So you're a news snoop, now. I might have known that a mealy-mouthed pacifist like you would end up peddling his ideas to the public. Cardiff, Samson, make sure you tie him up good. I don't want him getting away and causing more trouble."

"When my editor hears about this - "

"Your editor can shove it. This is a military operation and will be handled as such. I had enough of your news correspondent tactics when I was trying to protect our country's ideals in Vietnam."

"But if I don't report back soon, my editor will start wondering what happened - "

"I'll send him your obituary."

I was already eight feet deep in a six-foot hole, but I tried one last resort. "General, I think your actions may seriously affect our chances at future negotiations with the aliens."

"The only thing I'm going to negotiate with is this," he said, stooping down and picking up a stick of dynamite.

"What are you going to do?" I shouted, clawing at the tent flap as I was being pulled through.

"I'm going to blow up that mountain next to the saucer, and bury them under ten thousand tons of rock. I'd like to see them fight their way out of *that*."

"It'll never work."

"It had better work, Whitmore, because if it doesn't, we have instructions to drop an atom bomb on them at dawn. One way or another, we'll get them - before they get us."

The conversation ended when Cardiff and Samson - I didn't know who was who - hoisted me out of the tent by the armpits. I continued to shout imprecations about the power of the news media and the freedom of the press, but to no avail.

I was dragged into an adjacent tent in which Sergeant Kirk sat placidly at a desk surrounded by field radio equipment. The rest of the forty-foot-long tent was piled high with boxes of equipment: ammunition, grenades, flak vests, clothing, medical supplies, and gas masks.

Cardiff and Samson communicated their orders to Kirk. Since there were no real buildings in which I could be adequately locked, he suggested that I be tied to the central tent pole. My wrists were roughly bound together around the pole, with very little slack. But I must have looked too comfortable to them, for they then bound my legs around the pole with just enough rope so that I could stand up, but short enough that I couldn't stand up for very long. And when I sat, I was forced to bend my knees up to my chin. Not only was it uncomfortable, it was unglamorous.

After I was secured to their satisfaction, Cardiff and Samson departed. I redirected my abusive diatribe to Kirk until he calmly warned me that further complaint would be dealt with severely. He threatened to shove a potato in my mouth to keep me quiet. I quickly understood the rationale of silence.

For a while, I listened to the sound of troops loading trucks as the last of the dynamite was taken out of the neighboring tent. When the work was completed, the trucks roared off and the hubbub of the camp died down to an eerie somnolence.

Kirk was imperturbable. He seemed unconcerned that there was an alien spaceship resting only a couple of miles away, and that it was about to be buried under half a mountain of rock - or that none of his troops might return from the mission alive. I could easily picture this same cool personality writing out memos in a rice paddy while incoming rockets exploded mere feet away. When he was not answering calls or issuing instructions on the radio, he was filling out disposition forms for the materiel in the tent or making entries in the official log.

Meanwhile, I developed a plan of escape. Unfortunately, because of the pole my arms were wrapped around, I could not reach the penknife in my pocket. Strain as I might, there just was not enough slack in the rope.

The next obvious thing to do was to lift up the tent pole and slide out from under it. There was a snag here, too, in that the pole fitted into a broad metal base some two feet in circumference. I guess the base prevented the pole from sinking into the sandy ground, but it also thwarted my jailbreak.

I proceeded in one direction, however, while I searched for a possible loophole. In a quiet voice, so as not to get on Sergeant Kirk's nerves, I let known my desire to reach my editor with my story. It not only threw him off the track of my real intentions, but served to cover up any noise I might make while moving around the pole surveying the tent for possible escape routes.

When I finally stumbled on the best plan, it was right under my nose - literally. As I rose to my full height to stretch my cramped limbs, I noticed that the ten-foot aluminum tent pole was actually two sections, one of which fit into the other and was held in place by a cotter pin.

In between sentences, during which Kirk steadfastly ignored me, while he hunched over his desk with his back toward me, I gripped the pin with my teeth and little by little, with both hands lifting the upper section enough to relieve the downward pressure, pulled it out. In short order I was able to remove it and, with a jerk of my head, spit it onto the ground.

But my task was far from successful completion. Between the weight of the canvas and the tension of the guy ropes on the outside pegs, I could not lift the pole more than a quarter inch. Besides that, the aluminum was binding in the insert.

I rested for a minute before resuming my effort, shuffling my feet to make consistent covering noises. Then I tried again, twisting the pole as I lifted to ease the friction. I managed to get the pole halfway out of the dowel before I ran out of strength.

I sat down for fully five minutes, ticked off in thousands in my head, before I rose for another attempt.

With renewed effort, I grasped the pole and twisted and pushed upward. It went easily at first, but stopped when the pole was a mere half-inch from leaving the dowel.

Kirk must have sensed my strained breathing, for he suddenly turned around and saw what I was doing. I couldn't lift the pole another millimeter and was about to admit defeat. Kirk's eyes widened for a second in slow comprehension, and I knew that it was now or never. I fell backward with all my weight and pulled with my hands. It was enough pressure to break the pole out of the hole.

With tremendous force, the aluminum shaft dropped, slicing the air next to my head and catching my shoulder. I heard the tearing of fabric and felt the rending of flesh. But I did not have time to patronize myself.

As the tent collapsed, I rolled out of the way and squirmed across the floor so that my legs came free of the bottom pole. I saw Sergeant Kirk leaping toward me, but far short of his goal he was borne to the ground by collapsing canvas, crashing supplies, and radio equipment.

I fumbled my penknife out of my pocket and slashed my bonds, first the rope connecting my feet, then the one between my hands. The knots around my wrists and ankles would have to wait.

I jabbed the knife into the canvas and slashed open the material. Kirk was still cursing and struggling as I climbed through the hole. I clambered over boxes and crates and rolled across the dirt away from the tent.

Then I ran like hell.

Already the noise had attracted a small crowd of nearby soldiers. In the bright moonlight, I could see them converging on the site of the tent. In the middle of the huge pile of olive drab canvas, a bulging lump that was Sergeant Kirk was trying to fight his way out.

I hid in the shadows for a moment until I could see what I was looking for. Only thirty yards away, an army jeep sat unattended. When all the confusion was centered on the tent, I sped across the open ground, jumped into the driver's seat, pressed the starter button, and roared off. I switched on the headlights.

I was vaguely aware of some running figures behind me, yelling for me to halt. A moment later, I became acutely aware of a few wild and, I suspect, deliberately off-center shots fired over my head. I just ducked down and kept going. Shifting gears as fast as I could, I passed some dumbfounded sentries who foolishly tried to wave me down. They got out of the way a lot faster than they had gotten into it.

I barreled up the trail as fast as I dared, spitting sand from all four wheels. In minutes I came to a fork, one tine of which led south and out; the other dropped right into the ravine leading to the alien saucer. If the sergeant had been paying attention to my carefully constructed chatter, he would be sending a posse to the main road. I turned north and headed for the saucer.

Fifteen minutes later, I pulled the jeep over behind a boulder. I could not yet see the saucer, but its blue, coruscating glow lighted up a fair amount of sky. The aliens were not trying very hard to conceal their presence.

I cut away the rest of my bonds and rubbed my wrists and ankles where they had been rubbed raw. But they did not hurt half as much as my shoulder, where the tent pole had sloughed off a chunk of skin. I shrugged it off, for I had more important things on my mind.

Abandoning the jeep, I made my way on foot. I put each boot down like I was walking on glass. The moon was high overhead and so bright that it cast sharp shadows.

From a rise overlooking the wide valley where the saucer lay, I was able to take in the whole scene. The huge cliff overshadowed the bluely glowing saucer by five hundred feet. At the base of a short talus was a large pile of breakdown - from small rocks to boulders the size of a room.

If the aliens had been standing where I was, they

would have seen a long line of camouflaged soldiers sneaking through the rocks. Like a colony of ants, they formed an endless stream of workers, each carrying a box of dynamite on his back.

At first I couldn't understand how they had gotten the trucks so close to the saucer without being noticed. Then I saw a second contingent of soldiers *towing* a deuce-and-a-half with long ropes to a point just out of view from the saucer. From there the men had to carry the heavy boxes only a hundred yards over and through the boulder field.

The general, in typical military ignorance, was furthering the mistakes of his predecessors while exemplifying militaristic standards - shoot first and ask questions later. It's a great strategy if you're being attacked by a wild animal.

But the aliens were our intellectual superiors and there was no way I could ever believe that their intentions were hostile. True, I couldn't make sense out of the attack on the communications satellite, but I was willing to gamble that there was a logical explanation. I only hoped that I could make the general believe it.

As I walked ahead, my attention was riveted on that eerily glowing spaceship, the ship from the stars. I felt pity for them, for whatever was their purpose in coming here, they deserved more than an unprovoked attack by swarming hostile natives on an unfriendly foreign shore. I felt pity, too, for humanity, for our collective shortsightedness. The only thing we had to fear was the kickback from our own stupidity.

No one seemed to take particular notice of me as I merged with the hustling troops. I passed the truck that was being unloaded and walked calmly on, skirting around a man who was walking backward in a crouch, unreeling primacord that looked like clothesline from a wooden spool. I held my hands on the camera and canteen to keep them from swinging together around my waist.

Now there were no more men carrying dynamite: they were all returning empty-handed. And still no one challenged me; without giving me a second glance, they must have assumed that I had a right to be there. I reached the place where a veritable mountain of explosives had been piled. Only three men were left, crouched down behind the final rock curtain. Scarcely a hundred feet away, the alien saucer glowed quietly.

"Hey, you, get your ass down," came a whispered shout from the rocks. General Wordsworth stepped forward. "*Whitmore*, what the hell are you doing here?" he demanded, in language stronger than I am permitted to record.

If he expected an answer, he didn't give me much of a chance. In one easy motion, he lunged at me and buried a fist in my solar plexus. I folded up like an old accordion.

"You stupid fool, you'll get us all killed."

I groveled in the dirt, not gasping, not even breathing, while the three men continued the job at hand I was ignored.

"Goddammit, are you two finished yet?" growled the general under his breath.

"One more connection to make," said one of the Special Forces twins.

Enough tears had left my eyes so I could distinguish the green berets worn by Cardiff and Samson as they lay on the ground splicing primacord About five minutes later I took my first breath, and it hurt.

"Okay, it's all set."

"All right, then get going."

"What about him?"

"I'll take care of our newsy paperboy. You two trace this cord back and make sure there aren't any breaks in it. Spark the blasting cap from the battery of the truck we left at the top of the hill."

"What about you?"

"Don't you worry about me. You just blow that mountain as soon as you can. Hear?"

There was a moment's hesitation, then a muffled assent in unison. They scrambled off behind the rocks.

I was just starting to wheeze through bloodless lips

when the general said, "So you want to be a hero, do you? Well, by god, you're going to get your chance."

The general was decked out in full panoply, unbelievably carrying more arms and ammunition than he had carried before. In addition to hand grenades and bandoliers of M-16 rounds, he was also toting a forty-five on his hip and wearing a bullet-studded belt. He alternated his gaze between me and the open valley in front of the saucer. He seemed to have reached an attitude of calmness.

"Whitmore, I'm sorry you got yourself into this, but you asked for it. If I was a little rough on you, it's only because I have a job to do, and it's my duty to see that it gets done properly."

If I hadn't realized it sooner, I knew it now for certain. The general was handling the most dangerous part of the mission. He was literally sacrificing himself for his ideal - and I was going to be sacrificed along with him.

"General," I gasped, when I got enough breath back to speak. "Will you listen to me for a minute?"

Glancing at his wristwatch, he said, "You can say anything you want, but even you won't be able to talk your way out of this."

I nodded silently and took several deep breaths. My rib cage was sore, but not as sore as the patch of skin that had been torn off by the tent pole. I was in pretty bad shape, but I forced myself to ignore the pain.

Between coughs and gasps, I started the colloquy. "Do you know how advanced these beings must be in order to be able to cross the stars? Can you understand the kind of technology necessary to achieve such a thing? Can you imagine the sociological sophistication required of an intelligent race in order to handle that kind of power without killing themselves off? They must be so great, so far ahead of us in the evolution of the mind, that they view our bumbling, childlike civilization with disdain. They have at their control such power that there is nothing we can offer in retaliation."

The general's eyes passed over mine for a brief second, then returned to the saucer. But in that short time I saw a vision of the man. His eyes were blue and clear and ponderous, surrounded by a visage that was tough and stolid and beset with wrinkles. This man knew no fear. Or perhaps he knew it intellectually, but refused to acknowledge it emotionally. He peered out from under his helmet liner and steel pot, past the tip of his rifle, watching the blue glow of the saucer like a hen protecting her clutch of eggs from a fox. I was not even in the peripheral vision of his mind.

"General, what would you think if I told you that the aliens are peaceful; that they never attacked us - not once? Huhn, what would you think?"

"I'd think that you were refusing to recognize reality," he said, without ever moving his eyes.

"Then listen carefully to what I have to say." I forced myself to speak slowly and to enunciate each word properly, even though I knew that at any moment, a twelve-volt spark could end the conversation. "I can prove that the aliens never - not even once - made any aggressive action."

"You're gonna have to do some tall talking."

"All *I* have to do is point out the obvious. *You* have to distinguish when the obvious is being stated. Now, think about that tank crew and the man you pulled out of there. The aliens fired - excuse me - seemed to fire on the others. At least, they were all killed. But you and that other soldier were as exposed as they were, yet you escaped. Why?

"How about the helicopter assault on the saucer? Four choppers were blown to pieces, but two escaped. And the one that crashed was in full view of the saucer, but it was never fired upon. Why?"

By now I had the general's attention. He stared at me almost as if he was afraid I might make some sense.

"And what about that fighter squadron that got shot down. One of them escaped, didn't it? And why did it escape? Because its guns jammed, and since he didn't fire at them, there was no retaliation."

"Hell, I told you he was out of range."

"Now it's you who are not facing reality. If that saucer had the power to demolish two missile bases a thousand miles away, why couldn't it shoot down one more fighter plane? Huhn, tell me that."

"Then you tell me, mister smarty pants, why they shot down a harmless communications satellite?"

"No, General, *you* tell *me*. I'll admit that it had me puzzled at first, but I'm afraid that now I know the answer."

He looked at me blankly.

"Answer me, General."

"This is a hell of a time to play twenty questions. Face the fact that this is one story you'll never get to write, so what difference does it make?"

"Answer me," I nearly screamed.

"Pipe down, you fool, do you want to give us away?"

"Was it simply a harmless communications satellite," I answered for him, through gritted teeth, "or was it only *posing* as a communications satellite? Do we have orbital missile stations that are armed with nuclear warheads? And did one of them launch an automated attack on the saucer?"

"Whitmore, if you breathe a word of this I'll . . . "

I don't know what he was threatening, but with the grip he had on my collar, I wasn't sure I would ever breathe air again, much less than words. I grabbed his wrists and pulled his clenched fists away from my throat.

"Would you stop acting like a child who's just been told there's no Santa Claus? Think it out rationally. All they have is a force field - a big one protects their ship, smaller ones double as space suits and personnel protection screens. The force field keeps everything out - bullets, bombs, and poisonous atmosphere. At the same time, it prevents their own atmosphere from leaking out. It's a perfect system, for it allows them to go wherever they want without fear of harm, natural or otherwise."

"How does that explain our casualties?"

"The tank, the choppers, the fighters, the missile

bases, the satellite - they were all destroyed by the ricochet of the force of their own weapons. Every force that hits the alien screen is reflected back - like an equal but opposite reaction. This reflected energy takes the form of heat, and any resultant explosions are the result of this heat setting off other explosives, like the rockets and bombs carried by the choppers and the tank."

"It's a neat theory, but by the time you figure it out, you're already dead."

"Any truly peaceful civilization would never have opened fire on them. We have no one to blame but ourselves. If we're so damned backward that we greet strangers with physical violence, it just places us at the bottom of some intergalactic scale. Perhaps those who try to communicate are dealt with differently. Those who fight are ignored. If they die, it is by their own savagery. And we, thanks to our military preparedness, have shown them where we belong in the scheme of cultural evolution."

"All you've done is concoct an improbable story from circumstantial evidence. This saucer may represent an advance scout team sent to determine the effectiveness of our defenses."

"That's just your military mind accepting everything that is unknown as an act of aggression. Why don't you give them the benefit of the doubt?"

"Because they may slap our supplicating hand and knock us down. Even if the force field is only a defensive weapon, it enables them to go where they want and do what they want with impunity - like bank robbers wearing perfect armor. We can't afford to take that chance."

"You mean *you* can't afford to take that chance. *I'm* not afraid to take it." The general had long since relaxed his grip on my collar. I chose that moment to shove him aside and leap past him. I yanked out my penknife and, with one quick slice, severed the primacord between the dynamite and the detonator. Then I grabbed the end leading back to the truck and whipped it away and into the rocks.

"You crazy fool!" yelled the general, leaping at me with anger in his eyes.

I twisted out of the way, but his outstretched arms caught me and threw me to the ground. We groveled in the sand in a tangle of loose legs and swinging arms, punching, kicking, and - from the general - growling. I was at a disadvantage, for he was so protected by bandoliers of bullets and hand grenades that I did nothing more than bruise my knuckles.

I wrapped my arms around him and did my best to hold him tight. I don't know how long we rolled around in the dirt like two cowboys in a B-grade western, but I was nearly exhausted and about to give up when we tumbled over an edge and fell into the blue, eerie glow from the saucer.

Both of us stopped fighting, and for a moment the only sound was that of our labored breathing. In the same second, I realized that we were exposed to view. I heard the shuffle of rootlike feet on the ground, and saw moving shadows out of the corner of my eye.

When I looked up I saw six pairs - no, six triplets - of eyes staring down at us from a distance of less than fifty feet. A blue glow coruscated from the aliens' overhead jewels, limning the ravine in its unnatural color.

I lay paralyzed. I gulped a big lump in my throat. The general pushed away from me and slowly drew his forty-five.

"Don't shoot, if you value your life," I said.

He cocked the gun and drew a bead. He steeled himself for the worst.

"Your puny bullets are useless against the kind of force field that can repel an atomic explosion. If you pull that trigger, you'll only be killing yourself."

"I've got to do something, damn it. I can't die for nothing."

"General, you don't have to die at all. There is no threat. Don't you understand that they can't harm you even if they wanted to?"

The general was silent, but he chanced a suspicious glare at me.

"The force field is a perfect wall. Nothing can get in, nothing can get out. That translates as: you can't shoot them, they can't shoot you. If they tried to use a weapon against you, it would reflect back off the force field and kill them. It's a perfect defense mechanism that also prevents them from being an aggressor."

"I don't believe you."

"I'll prove it. Give me your gun."

He looked stunned for a moment, but did not resist when I pulled it out of his fist. He must have thought I was crazy.

I walked closer to the group of six, curious aliens. As before in the ravine, one of them aimed a device at me - probably a recorder. I trembled despite my braggadocio. I stared at those shields of blue light that offered such protection. Completely out of context, I wondered if one of those present was the one who had given me the canteen that still hung from my neck.

Slowly, I raised the pistol until it was aimed at a point just above their eye-stalked heads. With sweat pouring into my eyes, I pulled the trigger six times. Each blast was like the roar of a howitzer in that canyon, reverberating off the tall cliff face. But each succeeding shot was proof that they would not - could not - retaliate.

I dropped the gun-wielding arm to my side. Stalked eyeballs swung around wildly as if they were exchanging messages. While they were communicating in their bubble talk, I walked up to the nearest alien, the one with the device I assumed was a recorder. I pulled the camera off my neck by the strap, bent down and laid it on the ground in front of it. I never saw the alien pick it up, but somehow the force field moved over it and it mysteriously appeared in its hand. It bubbled to its companions, and all eyes swung around to me. Then of an accord, they zigzagged on their four oddly-jointed legs toward the spaceship.

Each alien's blue glow merged with the force field surrounding the saucer. I didn't see how they entered, but suddenly they were gone, absorbed into the superstructure of the strange craft.

I stood rooted to the spot, my heart beating almost normally. Then the general was standing beside me, staring at the pulsating blue shield. Even as we watched, the pulsing stopped and the dull blue grew to blinding brilliance.

With a whisper ever so slight, the saucer lifted off the ground. Slowly, but with increasing speed, it rose on a purple lambent flame, shrinking until it was the size of the moon. In seconds it was a tiny plum in the nighttime sky, then the bluish pinpoint of an electric arc, then nothing.

"You're either the biggest fool in the world, or the bravest idiot in or out of this man's army."

I think - or I would like to think -that he had faith in my theory of the aliens' divine benevolence. Else he would have have let me take his gun.

"But," said the general, removing the gun from my hand, and waving it in my face, moonlight glinting off its blued-steel barrel, "if they ever come back with the rest of their outfit, I'll personally hunt you down and blow your frigging head off."

He didn't grin, and I knew that he meant every word. But I didn't care, for in the end it was reason and humanity that prevailed. And General Wordsworth got the credit. I gave it to him. My account of the affair was published in every newspaper, magazine, and periodical in the world. Subsequent interviews were televised so often that Wordsworth became a household name, his face a widespread image.

General Wordsworth became famous, and I followed in the limelight of his glory.

The only thing that worries me is that blue shield. I'm no physicist, and I don't pretend to know anything about force fields. I just worked on the presumption that the aliens couldn't shoot through it from the inside. I mean - it makes sense. The general finally accepted it, albeit reluctantly. And later, I made the world believe it. But is it true?

I don't know. I can only hope - and pray. And wait.

SECOND BEGINNING

Jake woke up screaming.

In his mind's eye, he could still see the converging headlights, their bright beams spearing him like a pig on a spit. He could still hear the squealing tires rending the air with their awful, grating sound. He had been too tired and too scared to run. And with incredible swiftness the car bore down on him, at the last second swerving to avoid the inevitable collision - but too late.

He screamed again as the horrible memory wreaked havoc in his brain. Perhaps it was all a dream, he told himself. Perhaps I am having a nightmare.

But he knew all the while that he lied. The accident had happened. He had been hurt - and badly. He must be in the hospital.

The screaming died down to a low wail as he brought himself under control. Crying was not going to help. He must remain calm.

He tried to open his eyes but they were either covered with blood or swathed in bandages, for he was aware of nothing but shadows. Vaguely he remembered the tinkle of broken glass and the hiss of escaping radiator steam.

His body twitched spasmodically as he attempted to find muscular coordination. Nothing seemed to work right. He thought he could feel his hands grasping and his legs jerking, but nothing useful came of it. He could not move in any functional way.

Oh, my god, he screamed. I'm paralyzed!

He started screaming again, this time uncontrollably. His body did not feel pain, for he had no tactile sensations whatsoever. Instead, he lay there like a twitching, nerveless, laboratory specimen wired up to some Frankenstein electrical apparatus.

The real pain was in his mind: the pain of thought.

He did not know - *could* not know - what was wrong with him, or if he would ever recover. He feared the worst. It must be a broken spinal column or severe cerebral damage.

He let out another wail, but he was weakening. He tried to comfort himself with pleasant thoughts - if such were to be had. He tried to think about the good things in life: things like Marjorie, and the new house, and that rare stamp collection he had gotten for a song from his impoverished uncle-in-law. Technically he had only loaned the money to Uncle Frank with the stamp collection as collateral. But the proviso stipulated that if Frank did not come up with full payment within six months, the stamp collection would be his. And the six months would be up in another week.

Gradually his thoughts drifted toward more mundane things. How could he have been so stupid that he got hit by a car? For thirty years or more he had known enough to look both ways when crossing a street. It seemed such a childish mistake - but the results were so irreversibly grave.

He peeled back the layers of his memory, trying to reconstruct the events leading up to his thoughtlessness.

      *   *   *   *   *

Uncle Frank had called and asked us to come over because of some discoveries he had made in the early German collection. Marjorie decided to stay home. She was complaining of abdominal pains and, with the baby due in less than a week, she wanted to lie down to conserve her strength. I offered to stay with her but she said, no, it was all right, she just felt tired. If she needed anything, she promised to call me. After all, Uncle Frank lived only a few blocks away. She urged me to go for his sake: he was frightfully worried about his stamp collection. But I'm frightfully worried about the baby, I said.

Silly, she said, women have babies every day. But not this woman, and not this baby, I said. This baby is going to be someone special. Jake, please, she said, go to Uncle Frank's and leave me alone for a while. I'll be all right. Honest.

I finally consented and, with a parting smile, I petted her long black hair, tweaked her thin, aquiline nose, and kissed her forehead.

It was a clear, warm summer evening. The sun was low on the horizon and the sky was bathed in bands of red-streaked cirrus clouds. I walked the half-mile to Uncle Frank's, enjoying the sunset all the way.

"I thought you might not come," said Uncle Frank.

"Marjorie practically forced me out the door. I think she's tired of me hanging around and waiting on her. She doesn't seem to understand how exciting it is being a prospective father when you've never been one before. *I* think I'm just showing normal concern about the new baby."

"It's not really a new baby, you know," said Uncle Frank testily. He scratched his head under the great shock of snow-white hair. "Only the body is new. The soul is old and wise."

Sometimes I wished Uncle Frank had stayed in the seminary long enough to learn all the religious doctrines instead of coming away with the half-baked knowledge he seemed to possess. His theology lay somewhere between devout Catholicism and romantic mysticism. His personal intrusions combined the worst facets of both, leaving an ideology that confused religion with the occult. I really wasn't in the mood to hear any of his astrological prognostications.

"Call it what you will, this baby is still pretty important to me. All religious considerations aside, I feel as if it is an actual part of me which I am offering to the world. Since you never had any children of your own, it's something you can't possibly understand."

I couldn't help but throw a dig at him and his childless marriage, if only in anticipatory defense. He had married Connie soon after leaving the seminary (to tell the truth, he was kicked out because his beliefs were antagonistic) and I am sure it was only to have someone to wait on him. He was so wrought up about the purity of the mind, the soul, and the body, that I doubt if he had much of a sex life.

Switching onto another tack before he could riposte, I said, "Are you still going through the early German stamps?"

"Yes, and I found that they are more valuable than I thought. I've been checking the perforations and I've found that some of them are rarer than I suspected. And some of them are watermarked, which throws a completely different light on the matter."

The story was old and worn. For the past six months he had been telling me how much more the stamp collection was worth than I had paid for it. I couldn't figure out if he wanted more money, or if he expected me to hold off on confiscating it until he could afford to buy it back.

It was as if he was trying to make me responsible for his debts. If he had lost money in the grocery store, it was either because of his mismanagement or because he throttled his customers with his theological teachings so much that they found it far less draining to go farther afield to another grocery store where they could buy their products without a sermon. It was his luck that, in order to obtain his stamp collection, I was willing to pay off his debts so that the foreclosure proceedings on his house had been dropped.

Too, he knew as well as I that the book value of a stamp collection was unrealistically inflated. A stamp that cost a dollar might only retrieve a quarter or a dime on resale to a dealer. It was a true but unfortunate fact that a stamp collection for which one had paid thousands of dollars in the course of many years was, in the end, practically worthless on the open market.

The advantage to both of us was that I obtained stamps at a much-reduced rate rather than being ripped off by dealers, while he realized more money than he could have gotten from a dealer or at auction.

"That may be true, but a deal is a deal," I said, probably more cruelly than I should have. However, I had a notarized legal document locked in my safe deposit box backing up my statement.

("But he's my own uncle," Marjorie had complained. "Surely you don't think he would cheat you." "I know he won't cheat me because I'll have the paperwork to prove it. If he has no thought of reneging, it won't hurt him to sign the papers. Only the guilty at heart hesitate to do things legally.")

"I'm not suggesting that it isn't. I just thought you might see the unfairness of it to me. I mean, after all, you had me over the barrel."

"You had the choice of refusal."

"But my pecuniary predicaments required quick solubility."

"At least you didn't lose your house."

He paused for a moment to reconsider. "Jake, I was wondering if you might contemplate an extension of the repayment schedule. I'm anticipating an increase in the stock market, and in a few more months I expect to be more solvent. Of course, I would be willing to pay you interest for your good will."

I knew what stocks he had, and I knew that no matter what the stock market did, his stocks were not going to go up in value. One company had been off the board for months, and another recently declared chapter eleven. All the others were on the skids and did not even pay dividends. Uncle Frank had no one but himself to blame.

"Look, I've got a lot of things on my mind now. Couldn't we talk about it some other time? Maybe after the baby is born, we'll look at your stocks and see how they're doing."

"Well, if that's your attitude."

"It's not an attitude. It's called business acumen. Now, can I see those German stamps?"

"I've already got them out," he said in a huff.

Things were looking up for me. In four days, give or take a little, I would be a father. And in seven days, I would own this stamp collection. It galled me that I had to come to Uncle Frank's house to visit what I already considered mine.

We sat down at the kitchen table. The fixture dome had been taken off the overhead light so he could use forty-watt bulbs instead of hundreds, and the glare was disturbing.

I took out my wallet and laid it in front of me. I removed my perforation scale, pushed the wallet aside, and pulled the stamp album closer. It was already open to the proper page and I saw that he had made notations in pencil next to the indicated stamps.

One by one, I placed the scale alongside the stamps. Uncle Frank very efficiently laid a copy of Scott's Standard Stamp Catalogue next to me.

"Okay, so they are rare perforations," I admitted after a thorough examination. "But they're not worth *that* much more."

"Would you like the watermark detector?"

I hate the smell of lighter fluid, so I said, somewhat callously, "No, I'll take your word for it."

"Sometimes I don't think you have a soul," he said with a sneer on his face.

"I don't," I said bluntly. "I don't believe in the soul."

"Come now, surely you must acknowledge the fact that man is above the animal only by the possession of a soul."

"I believe that man is above the animal by the possession of greater intelligence, even though sometimes it is rather dismally displayed."

"Then what is it that lives on after you die - your intelligence?"

"Nothing lives on after I die. I revert to my component atoms like the rest of the animals. And plants too, for that matter."

"Jake, you are woefully wrong. Your intelligence may die, but your soul lives on forever."

"And where does it live? In heaven?"

"No, it is passed on from body to body. The essence that is you was at one time someone else. And before that it was someone else again."

"Then why don't I remember my previous self?"

"Knowledge cannot survive reincarnation. The pain

of birth sears the soul of all recollection of previous life."

"How can you go hopscotching from body to body? It's all too transcendental for me."

"If you had the faith, you would not fear death. You would be secure in the knowledge that life, in some form, would continue. If you try hard enough, even *you* could find comfort."

"I don't need comfort. I'm not afraid of death."

"You are indeed fortunate. However, it was that knowledge that helped me through Constance's miserable sickness and her eventual succumbing to death."

I'll just bet you needed comfort, I thought. I still have my doubts about the whole thing. According to the official verdict, Aunt Constance had gotten her pills confused. She had taken none of one medication and too much of another. But I always believed that she just couldn't stand to be around her whimpering husband any more. Either that or she died of sexual frustration.

"I know that she has safely passed onto a new existence. She may even sustain slight remembrances - dé·jà vu, if you will - of this life."

"Like in the case of Bridey Murphy," I stated flatly.

"That is one over-publicized example. There are many others. When your body fails in this world, your soul transmigrates to the nearest birthing child and establishes a new abode. And in the process, it loses the essence of its prior existence and must start anew."

"Sort of like musical chairs. When the music stops, the soul hotfoots it around looking for another seat."

The look on Uncle Jake's face warned me that I was overstepping my boundaries by treading on his theological toes too facetiously. But his comment died aborning, interrupted by the sudden and loud ringing of the wall phone.

He answered in the same gruff tone he would have used with me. A moment later, he handed me the phone, and said, "It's your wife."

"What's the matter, Honey?" I asked, grabbing the phone. I anticipated the worst.

"Oh, Jake, I didn't want to disturb you when you were with Uncle Frank."

"That's okay, Honey. Just tell me what's wrong."

"Well, you know those abdominal pains I was having?"

"Are they worse?"

"No, they're about the same. But they're more frequent now. You know, I never thought to time them before you left, but I think they must have been about twenty minutes apart. Now they're only ten minutes apart. I didn't want to call until I was sure, but I think the time may be soon."

How could that stupid doctor be off by four days? Didn't he know how to count? What the hell was I paying him for?

"Don't do a thing," I shouted into the mouthpiece. "I'll be right home."

I slammed down the phone and jumped out of the chair. To Uncle Frank, I said, "You can pray for my soul if you want, but I've got to get Marjorie to the hospital. There's another soul on the way."

I ran out the door before he had a chance to comment. Filled with exhilaration, I dashed up the street in the gloom. It was only half a mile to my house - five short blocks. I could jog it in five minutes.

Alas, I wasn't in the shape I used to be in. The desk job had slowly sapped the strength I used to have in college. My unused muscles had turned to flab, with a little paunch around the middle that added weight without stamina. After one block I was walking - and gasping for breath.

Sweat poured down my face and from under my armpits as my pace was reduced to a determined canter. Overhead lights spotted small oases in the dark. I counted each pole as I passed it, and told myself to keep running as far as the next one. The cumulative achievement of small goals would surely see me home.

I had only two blocks to go when I had a sudden realization. Desperately I felt in all my pockets, but they were empty. My wallet still lay on Uncle Frank's dimly-lit kitchen table.

I couldn't go back for it: my fatigue-racked body would never survive the additional strain. Perhaps I could swing by Uncle Frank's place on my way to the hospital - if Marjorie were not too far-gone.

One block away from home, the merest tenth of a mile, I had to stop to catch my breath. I leaned against a telephone pole on top of which was mounted a streetlight. It would do me no good to arrive home breathless.

Surging on, I stepped between two parked cars and made my way across the street. At the same time, a lone car rounded the corner and sped along the deserted street.

Momentarily I hesitated, not knowing whether to go ahead or to drop back. The car hesitated, too, decreasing in speed when the headlights picked me out in the middle of the street.

With the knowledge that the driver was aware of me, I decided to continue across the street. An instant later the car swerved in that direction. I half turned and took a step back, but again it veered my way. I was too exhausted to play cat and mouse, so I resolved to let the driver make the choice.

Relief came over me when the car passed beneath the streetlight a hundred feet away. I recognized Uncle Frank's maroon sedan. The old bastard had found my wallet and was bringing it to me.

High beams flashed on and blinded me. There was a screech of tires as he downshifted into second gear and stomped on the accelerator. The car turned to follow my half-hearted attempt to escape. I raised my arms defensively, finding grim humor even in the throws of death at my instinctive effort to stop two tons of moving steel.

The bumper caught my shins about a split second before the hood ornament ripped open my stomach. I was lifted bodily off the ground, and as I flew through the air toward oblivion, I had a last clear look at Uncle Frank's leering face.

*   *   *   *   *

Jake screamed again, and for a moment the pain was real. But like all pain, it faded rapidly.

He struggled convulsively. A strange hunger gnawed at his vitals. The pain was gone, and the memory of it but a dream. The incidents leading up to his accident passed into unreality.

The street became a dim recollection. The horrible pain and physical rending was obliterated from his mind. He could not even remember his name.

He felt comfortable at last, with a feeling of both outer and inner warmth. As his eyes grew accustomed to the surrounding brightness, he chanced a peek through clenched eyelids. His heart and soul and body were lifted into the air and cuddled with love and understanding. There were no more bad thoughts.

Through filmy eyes, he caught a glimpse of a vaguely familiar face: it had a sharp, pointed nose and was embraced by long, dark curls. And in the distance stood an old man with a great mop of white hair. But he did not know them.

All experience vanished. Knowledge disappeared with ever quickening speed. His mind became a blank in which even the process of thought was nonexistent. He knew nothing.

Something soft and moist and yielding was gently pushed into his mouth. He stopped screaming, and discovered how to suck the precious fluid that would satisfy his hunger.

It was the end of pain. It was a new beginning.

IN HIS STEAD

Professor Mead sat alone in his cell.

He had been put into solitary confinement, not because of anything he had done wrong within the prison system, but because he had requested it after an incident with his cellmates.

Professor Mead learned the hard way that convicts in the mid twenty-first century were no more civilized than their predecessors of the previous century.

A naive and even-tempered man, he had reacted violently when the three men with whom he shared his cell made lewd suggestions. When it occurred to him that they were not joking as they ran their grimy hands over his body, he struck out blindly, punching one of them in the face. But he was no match for the three of them. They held him down and carried out a long, aggravated assault on his body until he was bleeding from a dozen wounds. And although he fought like a wildcat, they got him in the end.

By the time the guards intervened, Professor Mead's body was a mass of blood and bruises, and he had sustained several broken ribs as well. He was admitted to the prison hospital for treatment. When he was released several days later, he requested a cell by himself.

It was not prison policy, however, to accede to prisoners' requests. He was dutifully placed in a different cell with three other inmates who were, in the professor's own words, hopeless criminals. He thought he deserved better. To prove his point, he started a ruckus and finally had to be dragged out bloody and bruised for another trip back to the hospital.

This time, when he was released from medical care,

they *did* put him in solitary. And from then on, he knew that this was where he wanted to spend the next five years, until he was due for parole.

To most it was dank, dark, and somber. But to the professor it was freedom of the mind, a place where he could dream, and think, and plan his revenge.

And so he pleaded and begged the authorities to let him stay. Finally, they agreed.

Any day now, he expected to be released.

    *   *   *   *   *

The new guard had been working in the New York State Penitentiary for little more than a week. At first he had doubled up with an older, more experienced guard who had shown him the routine of night duty. He proved an apt pupil and quickly mastered his itinerary, entering each cellblock with the clipboard and checking off each name. He had done so well that tonight he was told to make the twelve o'clock rounds by himself, while his mentor sat in the cafeteria drinking coffee.

Brushing up his uniform and tipping down the peak of his hat, he let himself into cell block three and, as he had been instructed to do, closed and locked the heavy steel door behind him. He carried a billy stick on his hip and a clipboard in his hand. The roster had been printed that evening. The midnight call should have found every prisoner in his assigned cell.

As he called out their names, the men acted gruffly, for they did not like being wakened. Most of them, of course, just pretended to be asleep for the fun of it. Sensory input was at a premium for long-term jail birds. Occasionally, he had to rap on the bars with his billy stick to get one's attention.

From cell to cell he went, calling off names, checking the list with his pencil. When he reached cell number twenty-two, he paused for a long moment, staring at the inmates. All four men appeared to be asleep.

"Johnson," said the guard quietly. There was no response. "Johnson," he said louder. Two of the men rolled over, mumbling. "Johnson," he repeated for the third time.

"Yeah," I'm here," growled a coarse voice.

"Johnson," said the guard evenly.

"I'm here, I said," grumbled the prisoner without opening his eyes.

"Johnson," repeated the guard, not in exasperation but in demand.

"I'm here, goddamn it. Now leave me alone."

"Come here, Johnson."

Johnson sat up in his bunk, squinting, for this was a circumstance out of the ordinary. "Whaddayawant?"

"Come over here."

Almost in disbelief, Johnson slowly rose from his bunk and approached the cell door barefooted. He acted like a well-trained automaton, and looked at the guard blankly.

"Johnson, do you remember Professor Mead?"

Johnson was shocked for a minute. After screwing up his eyes and thinking, he said, "You mean that rabbit-sized guy with the big ears?" Johnson's face split into a huge grin. "Yeah, I remember him. That was a long time ago. Coupla years. Maybe more. We had some fun with him before he got out. Why?"

The guard reached into his shirt and removed a long-barreled pistol adorned with a bulbous, black silencer.

"The professor sends his greetings."

He aimed the gun at Johnson, right between and slightly below the beady eyes. The tiny whoosh grossly belied the force behind the bullet as it crashed through the soft cartilage of the nose, passed through the nasal cavity, and entered the brain. Before Johnson's body slumped to the floor, the guard had replaced the gun in its underarm holster and was halfway to the steel door that closed off cell block three.

He closed the door gently as he left.

*   *   *   *   *

"All we know is that he applied about a month ago, took the examination, got moderately high scores, and we hired him. His credentials at the time seemed sufficient. He started working last week, learned quickly, and was given his first time running the rounds solo. After he killed Johnson, he reported to his duty officer, turned in his roster, and walked out of the prison. He hasn't been seen or heard from since."

The warden ran a manicured hand through his prematurely gray hair, and scratched an imaginary itch. Bob Droyd, the state investigator sitting opposite him, thoughtfully rubbed his chin.

Droyd understood what embarrassment the warden was suffering. Everything that happened in the State Pen was his responsibility, whether he was to blame or not. But blame didn't matter to Droyd. He was here to investigate, not to censure.

"I don't know any more than that," insisted the warden.

"I understand your position and I sympathize with you. I will be satisfied if you will authorize your computer to file a formal report of all details with my office."

Droyd had already interrogated the prisoners in cell block three, and had come up with exactly nothing. No one had seen the incident; no one had heard a gun shot. One of Johnson's cellmates thought he heard a squishing sound, like a rotten tomato trampled underfoot. He was wakened by the falling body, and when he tried to rouse Johnson, he found the back of his head gone and blood smeared all over the back wall of the cell. Then he began to scream.

"I would appreciate it also if you will have your computer transfer Johnson's dossier to the Police Central Computer. I want the transcript of his trial, his psychiatric reports, and everything known about him since he entered this prison."

"Sure, Mr. Droyd, that's no problem. I'll have one of my technicians cross-index our records right away. You should have it no later than this afternoon. Uh, look, I'm in kind of a bind here. Nothing like this has ever happened before, and unless you catch that guy, I'm in big trouble. What are the chances?"

"Five years ago I would have said nil. His name, address, and social security number are all false. His fingerprints are not on file. A quick computer check cn his job application photo has turned up nothing. So far, he is a nonentity."

"Then what do you have to go on?"

"A relationship in the past which links him with Johnson. That is why I need everything that is known about him, so the Police Central Computer can cross-reference the information and come up with a probability index of possible suspects. In the five years since its institution, it has solved much more nebulous mysteries. I am confident that it will do the same in this case."

"I sure hope so," said the warden grimly. "I sure hope so."

*   *   *   *   *

Forty miles away, at the state minimum security prison, the inmates were coming in from the fields after a hard day's work in the broiling sun. Scores of men dressed in prison fatigues were wiping their hands cn their trousers and anticipating a cool shower and a hardy dinner. Several guards stood around the gate shooing them in.

When there were only a few stragglers left outside, one of the guards said to the others, "Go ahead in fellows, I'll wait for the rest." The guards went through the gate and into the single-story building to handle the job of getting the prisoners into the proper cubicles.

"Hold up there, you," said the remaining guard to one of the returning men. With a strong right hand, he pulled the man aside. His companions and cellmates glanced away and filed in silently.

"What's up?" asked the prisoner in consternation

When the two of them stood alone outside the brick wall, the guard said, "I've got a message from Professor Mead."

Before the prisoner had time to react, or even to understand what he had heard, the guard drew a shiny blued pistol. In one short staccato burst, he fired six slugs into the prisoner's groin. While he grabbed what had once been his genito-urinary system, the guard holstered the gun and ran like the blazes.

The noise attracted a squad of uniformed guards as well as a horde of curious inmates. A short pursuit was made while the fatally injured prisoner screamed in wretched agony, but the recalcitrant guard demonstrated unheard of athletic skills, bounding over bushes and dodging trees with amazing celerity.

He escaped into the setting sun.

*   *   *   *   *

Bob Droyd was still putting information on the Johnson murder into the Police Central Computer when he received word of the killing of Anderson Hays at the State Minimum Security Prison. He was about to put the investigation in the hands of an underling when he noticed the similarity of the circumstances.

Despite what Droyd had told the warden, there were unsolved cases on the books that even the computer could not help clarify. Just as a ship at sea needs more than one vector in order to triangulate its position, the computer needed corroborative evidence on two or more points to arrive at a solution. Otherwise, it could do no more than indicate areas of high probability.

Unfortunately, his interview at the minimum security prison proved inconclusive. The modus operandi was identical: the guard was new, and was on the job for the first day; his identity had been completely falsified; death was quick and decisive, if unnecessarily brutal. But a simple comparison of the guard's application and identification papers - taken by the hiring board - showed different photos and fingerprints.

The crimes were the same, but the perpetrators were different.

Droyd was confused. Yet, somewhere in the histories of the two dead men, there must be a common denominator. He placed an immediate order for Hays's dossier, locked himself into the police computer room, and punched in the information as it arrived. Somewhere there was a correlation, and if he had to stay up all night to find it, he would.

So far, the only evidence he had that was outstanding was the almost miraculous escape of the guard.

　　　*　　　*　　　*　　　*　　　*

The courtroom was cool, quiet, and somewhat somber. The main witness for the prosecution had just left the stand and the evidence weighed heavily against Arnold.

His lawyer was a state appointed volunteer: young and fresh out of law school. Even so, he exhibited qualities that were both bold and confident.

But boldness and confidence would not get Arnold off the hook. After three prison terms, there was little doubt that he was about to face another.

"As it is near the noon hour," intoned the judge, "I suggest that we break for lunch and resume court at one-thirty."

"All rise," called the bailiff, as the judge left the courtroom in a sweep of flowing robes.

The guard walked up from the double doors at the back of the room and went directly to the table of the accused. Arnold turned away from his lawyer and, seeing the blue uniform approaching, perfunctorily held out his hands for the cuffs.

"Hey, where's Harry?" he asked in surprise.

"Went home sick," said the guard, looking up at Arnold's six-foot figure. He snapped on the handcuffs and led the prisoner along the aisle and out the door. His lawyer sighed resignedly, but not gloomily. After all, he might lose his first case, but at least he would not go to jail for it.

The courthouse was only moderately crowded and few people got in their way as Arnold and his guard walked along the hall to the holding cell, where Arnold would remain until court reconvened. They were halfway there when someone shouted from behind.

"Hold that man, I want to speak with him."

Both guard and his ward turned and saw, coming toward them, a plainclothes detective. Bob Droyd had just run up the long marble steps from the lobby of the courthouse. He slowed to a walk and approached the two men with equanimity.

"Pardon me, guard, but I would like to have a few

words with this man. I am state investigator Droyd, and I have reason to believe that his life is in danger."

Without preamble, the guard lashed out at Droyd with a backhanded fist that crashed into his head and knocked him against the tiled wall. There was no blood, but the guard's fist had left a sizable dent in the side of Droyd's head.

"Hey, what's going on?" shrieked Arnold.

With the same hand with which he had felled the investigator, the guard shoved Arnold away. Reaching into his shirt, he pulled out a sleek pistol and shot him three times through the heart. If the short tussle and scream had not alerted bystanders, the reverberating blasts captured everyone's horrified attention.

"Stop that man," Droyd yelled from his position on the floor, shaking his head but not yet recovered from the blow to his skull.

Two policemen were already charging down the corridor with drawn weapons. They saw Arnold's still writhing body on the floor, the fleeing guard, and Droyd's pointing finger.

"Halt, or I'll shoot," shouted one of them, leveling his gun.

With phenomenal speed, the guard raced down the hall toward the fire-escape door. He showed no inclination of slowing down.

The policeman who had called, waited two seconds, then fired two shots over the fleeing guard's head. The bullets gouged holes in the woodwork above the door. One second later, the guard smashed into the door and, with lowered shoulder, ripped the door off its hinges with a terrible crash.

The other policeman took quick aim and emptied his gun at the guard's back as he disappeared down the stairs.

"Damn, Fred," said the policeman who had fired high. "You better get some more practice at the range. You missed him six times."

"Missed him hell. He musta been wearing a bullet-proof vest."

"The way he was running, you'd a thought it was goose down."

No one even bothered to mention the obvious - that he had knocked a thick, oaken door off its mount and splintered the wood.

*   *   *   *   *

"I'm sorry to disturb you, Mr. Hanover, but it is rather important."

Bob Droyd introduced himself and showed his authority punch cards. He pushed his way into Bruce Hanover's plush office on the one hundred fiftieth floor of the Hanover Building, the headquarters of Planned Mechanicals, Inc. Without waiting for courtesy, Droyd claimed a chair opposite Hanover's desk.

"I'm not used to seeing people unannounced and without an appointment," said Hanover brusquely, walking stiffly around Droyd to his own leather chair.

It was long after office hours, but it was not unusual for Hanover to stay late and keep some of his immediate personnel with him. "This is quite out of order."

"I'm sure it is," replied Droyd evenly. "Nevertheless, it is dire necessity that brings me here."

"And what is of such dire necessity - to me, that is, and not to you - that it couldn't be handled by my secretary in the routine manner, Mr. . . . Mr. . . . uh . . . ?"

"Droyd," supplied the investigator. "Just as it says on my card. Perhaps you would like one for your file," he said, removing a small business card from a pocket and passing it to Hanover."

"Yes, Mr. Droyd," said Hanover, taking the card but not looking at it. "And why can't this matter be handled by my secretary?"

"Because it is *your* life that is at stake, Mr. Hanover," said Droyd softly.

Hanover was visibly taken aback. "Is this some kind of a joke?"

"I am in deadly earnest, if you will pardon the play on words," said Droyd. "I have strong reason to believe that an attempt will be made on your life this very night."

Hanover leaned back in his chair, nonplussed. "But who would want to kill me? I don't have any enemies."

"Don't be naive, Mr. Hanover. A businessman without enemies is a contradiction in terms."

"I admit that I have competitors, Mr. . . . uh . . . " and here Hanover glanced at Droyd's business card. "Mr. Droyd. After all, competition is an accepted business ethic."

"Someone within your own company, perhaps?" suggested Droyd. "Someone who no longer works for you?"

Hanover knitted his eyes for fully ten seconds, staring straight into the depths of Droyd's prismatic orbs. "Surely you don't mean Professor Mead?"

"The same."

"But he's in jail for embezzlement and computer theft," said Hanover, using the phrase "computer theft" as a catchall for the many and various forms of misappropriation of funds, services, and materials committed criminally by false programming. It was a necessary and much needed legal concept.

"He *was*," Droyd corrected. "He obtained parole about a year ago and has not been seen nor heard from since. The parole board has listed him as having broken bond. He has disappeared into the multitude of anonymity."

"Probably on money that he embezzled from my company."

"I cannot comment on that, Mr. Hanover."

Hanover scowled and paused to ruminate before he spoke again. "What makes you think that after a year among the rolls of the missing, he will choose tonight to make a bid for revenge?"

"Because in the past three days there have occurred three deaths which led me to this conclusion."

"Three deaths?" exclaimed Hanover in astonishment.

"Please, let me explain. Although you might think of me as a detective, I am really a computer programmer. It is true that I handle investigative work but that is merely to collect information for the Police Central Computer. You need know nothing more about the three previous deaths other than that they were murders committed by an unusual type of man, and that the victims all shared a cell with one Professor Mead - and that they had all done him harm."

Droyd paused dramatically. Hanover, he noticed, was sweating profusely. Wiping his brow with a monogrammed handkerchief, he said, "Do you think Professor Mead wants to murder me because of . . . ?" His voice trailed off in a meaningless stutter.

"Because of your testimony at his trial. Although I am certain that he would have been convicted in light of the physical evidence presented to the court, your statements were additionally damaging to his character. It may not have weighed heavily against the court, but it *did* weigh upon his mind."

"How do you know all this, Mr., uh, Droyd?"

"I am sure that in your present circumstances, you are unaware of modern police technology. For several years now, we have been using a central computer system to correlate facts turned up during an investigation. We program into the computer not only the deeds of a crime, but also all physical and psychological information about all persons involved in it. The computer then digests everything and cross-indexes probability lines and, more often than not, divulges a probable solution. In today's complex and high-speed world, it is the only way we can cope with the criminal mind.

"The first murder was cleverly constructed and left us with only a low probability profile which would have taken time to untangle. By the time the second murder had been committed and all the information computed, I knew for certain the name of the murderer, as well as his motive. Unfortunately, I did not find this out in time to prevent the third murder, which took place right in the courthouse under the eyes of scores of witnesses."

"I always knew that Professor Mead was eccentric - even brilliantly eccentric. But I never thought he'd have the kind of guts it takes to kill a man in public and think he could get away with it."

"You are quite right in that respect, Mr. Hanover."

"What do you mean?"

"I mean that from his personality profile, the computer predicted two very important items which I was unable to interpret properly at the time. One was that he would never do anything to endanger his own life or freedom, and the other was that he would perform any deed in such a clever manner that eventual capture would be extremely problematical."

Hanover had calmed down considerably during Droyd's rational explanation, and it was obvious that the investigator had succeeded in putting him at ease.

"But how does that coincide with what you just told me about these murders?" Hanover asked shrewdly.

"Professor Mead did not personally commit the murders."

"You mean he hired killers?"

"Not exactly. You see, another correlation that came out of our computer search was his position with Planned Mechanicals, Inc. Professor Mead was considered a genius in the fields of electronics, mechanics, and cybernetics, which was why he served you so well as head of your research and production departments. Before his incarceration, he developed some rather radical designs in the realm of humanoid, general purpose, self-regulating mechanical units controlled by responsive, automatic feedback computer processors. To use a somewhat derogatory but all-encompassing term - robots."

"Professor Mead's genius was overemphasized, but his radicalism was grossly understated. He was a nut with delusions of grandeur. He was pouring company funds into research programs that were not only unrealistic, but which, if they had succeeded - which they never could have - would have served no useful purpose."

"I understand that it was Professor Mead's goal to build mechanical units of extensive longevity by utilizing finely machined parts, designing highly efficient components, and integrating self-servicing mechanisms."

"All of which is like pouring money down the drain. We build human looking mechanical units merely as a cosmetic because people can work with them better. No one wants to work with or look at a walking, talking, response-integrated computer that has gears and wires protruding from its abdomen. Mechanicals are nothing more than workhorses: you use them until they're out of date or not worth repairing, then you throw them out. You don't build them like Rolls Royces."

"In other words, your mechanicals operate on the principle of built-in obsolescence." It was a statement rather than a question.

Hanover harrumphed. "That's life in big business. Unless you're suggesting that we build according to substandard levels just so we can increase production?"

"I make no suggestions, only observations."

"And excellent observations they are," said a strange voice. A short, loosely clad man stepped into the room waving a dangerous-looking pistol. "You have my commendations, Mr. Droyd. Surely I am up against a better man than I suspected the police department would have in their employ."

Hanover literally jumped out of his soft, leather chair, but Droyd remained calm.

"Ah, Professor Mead, I'm afraid you give me too much credit. It is not I who am your nemesis, but the Police Central Computer. I am only its investigator."

"Whatever you call yourself, your prowess has done nothing more than to endanger your own life - if you choose to get between me and my purpose."

"You have me at a disadvantage, Professor."

"You can't let him kill me," screamed Hanover, backing into a corner and making ineffectual warding motions with his hands.

"I seem to be powerless to stop him, Mr. Hanover."

"I'm glad you feel that way," cautioned Mead. "You may very well leave here with your life."

"I react according to reason, Professor Mead, not to emotion. Unfortunately, this time reason has let me down. I expected you to send one of your rather impressive mechanicals to do away with Mr. Hanover, as you did with your former cell mates."

"I suspect your computer has much to learn about human motivation. I was content to have those unworthy men killed out of hand, for they violated only my body. But Bruce Hanover violated my mind and my freedom of will. He must be made to suffer - at my own hands."

Hanover continued to cower in the corner. Now a thin stream of saliva crept out of one corner of his mouth.

"Get away from me, Mead, you crazy man."

"That's what I wanted, dear Hanover. I want to hear you plead."

"I'll plead, if that's what you want," cried Hanover. "I can give you money, too. How much do you want?"

"More than you've got. More than you could ever pay me. Because your money won't do me any good. I never wanted your money, all I wanted was to produce. I didn't care if my work made you rich, as long as I had the opportunity to create. I could have made the best mechanicals in the world if you had let me. But you didn't want anything too perfect for fear it would have diminished sales and ruined repair service. So you framed me for computer theft and had me sent to jail. That is why I must kill you. But first, I had to see you plead for mercy, to show you up for the coward that you are. And now that you have met so admirably with my expectations, you can die."

The wavering gun was slowly brought up to eye level and made to bear on Hanover's head. The terrified businessman squeezed tighter into the corner, with tears of fright streaming from his eyes, and cried, "Don't shoot me, don't shoot me. I'll beg for my life if that's what you want, but don't kill me."

Bob Droyd, however, was not idle. He had been calmly waiting for the opportunity to act, and now was going to be the last opportunity he would have before Hanover's demise. Reacting with speed that was barely less than astronomical, he leaped out of his chair with such force that it flew backward into the wall and was broken into splinters. Like a streak of lightning, he grabbed the professor's gun-gripped hand and shoved it aside just as lead and flame erupted from its snout.

In one easy, wrenching motion, he relieved the professor of his gun. Then, with a strength belied by his calm appearance, he picked Professor Mead up off the ground and held him aloft in the air in outstretched arms.

The professor squirmed and kicked like a child in tantrum. But Droyd held him firmly off the floor until two uniformed policemen, alerted by the blast of the gun, entered the office and took him off his hands.

They dragged him out screaming, "Let me go. Let me kill him. I want him to die for sending me to prison in his stead." His shouted curses reverberated off the walls until they were silenced by the closing elevator doors.

Hanover was a long time regaining his composure. He climbed out of his corner, reseated himself at his desk, and wiped his face and forehead with his already soaked handkerchief. The bullet had missed him by scant inches.

"I'm sorry if I was abrupt with you . . . I mean, I didn't know . . . that is, when you first got here . . . I'm sorry . . . I really must thank you for what . . . "

"That's quite all right, Mr. Hanover. No apologies or thanks are necessary. It is an unpleasantness that is all in a day's work."

Hanover found a dry handkerchief in his desk and went over his face again. "You know, you really had me fooled. I mean, I didn't even see you move. Where did you get such reflexes - and such strength?"

"From Professor Mead."

"What? What are you talking about, Mr. . . uh . . ."

"My name is on the card I gave to you earlier, and if you will look closely, you will find that my middle initial is 'N.' Professor Mead is indeed a genius in his field."

"You mean . . . "

"Yes, Mr. Hanover, I am one of his creations, and one of your products. I have Professor Mead to thank for my innovations, and you to thank for my limitations."

"What do you mean by that?"

"I was put together for your inspection as a pre-production model. And although I am built to close tolerances and rigid specifications, if Professor Mead had been allowed to continue his work, improvements would have been forth-coming that he could have incorporated into my body as well as in the proposed new line of mechanicals. Instead, he went to jail, and I went to auction to keep the company solvent after its financial deficits. I was sold for a paltry sum that was far beneath my talents, eventually to find my way to the police department, where I was put to work with the incumbent Police Central Computer with which I have much in common. And so I am stuck with a body that is in constant need of minor repairs and replacement parts. I must be put into the shop for periodic maintenance. And my atomic batteries are so drained by inefficient servo-mechanisms that they must be recharged every year. It is your greed that is the cause of it all."

"Now, see here. I won't be talked to this way - especially by one of my own machines. Remember, I own the company that built you."

"I meant no disrespect, Mr. Hanover. I was just defining reality. Any antipathy you feel is justified by truth. *I* am not the maker of that truth, only its bearer. Now, if you would be so kind as to accompany me to the police station?"

"Can't it wait until morning?" said Hanover, somewhat put out at Droyd's intricate observations. "This has all been rather exhausting and I would like to go home to bed. I'll stop in tomorrow to make my report."

"You do not understand, Mr. Hanover. I am not asking you to make a report. I am placing you under arrest."

"What!" Hanover screamed. "What are you talking about now?"

"You are forgetting the computer. When it predicted from trial testimony and personality files that Professor Mead was so brilliant, so analytical, and so methodical, that had he committed the computer theft for which he had been accused, there was a ninety-eight point seven percent chance of its success, I was forced to reprogram the evidence in the case. Since you testified at the hearing, your dossier was on file. The computer picked out your predilection toward gambling and suggested a new line of investigation with you as the prime suspect. I am now in the process of requisitioning the financial statements of Planned Mechanicals during the time of the theft, as well as your personal income tax reports and bank accounts. That, I am certain, will cinch the case. And since there is no statute of limitations on crimes of felony, I now charge you with fraud, embezzlement, and computer theft of your own company."

"But you can't do this . . . you can't get away with . . . " Hanover sputtered uselessly.

"Mr. Hanover, a little while ago, it was my unhappy duty to arrest Professor Mead, a job which I found embarrassingly distasteful. Now, however, I can perform a task which is more to my liking. You see, I admire Professor Mead, and I despise you. He might have built mechanicals that could live forever, but you stopped him. So the next time I am laid up for repairs, I can remember this moment with fondness. Now, if you will please accompany me to the station?"

Resignedly, Hanover let himself be led away.

*　　*　　*　　*　　*

Professor Mead was indeed a genius in his field. But even *he* did not possess the messianic abilities that Droyd attributed to him.

Forty-six years passed before his spry form encountered the vicissitudes of aging. He had been a healthy and uncomplaining figure for so long in the prison system that he had been accepted as a permanent fixture. When he developed a short circuit in one of the selenium cells that controlled his motor coordination, he was carried off to the hospital in all due haste.

What the doctors uncovered, to the surprise of all, was a humanoid mechanical that needed repair instead of prescription or surgery. But by then, there was nothing the authorities could do about it, for the real Professor Mead had died quietly in his sleep some ten years earlier, after a long life and happy retirement.

Until his passing he had received without fail, yearly Christmas greetings and birthday cards from his long-time friend and cohort, one Robert N. Droyd.

THE MIND'S EYE

I can't see any more since they took away my eyes, but I can remember what it was like.

The world was a live and lovely place, and it glowed with a prismatic warmth that melted into the soul of all those who were sensitive enough to appreciate it. There were brown rolling hills and fields of green dewy grass and forests of tall sturdy trees with crackling leaves that fluttered in the evening breeze. Mountains rose majestically into the bold blue sky while white puffs of clouds floated lazily high overhead.

Yet, people were unhappy.

I can still taste the wind as it whispered through quaint country towns that pulsed with life and sang the melody of laughter . . .

. . . and the groan of suppression.

I can smell, although dimly, the freshness of flowers blooming in springtime and the invigorating staleness of manure in the stables. I can remember all that was good in the world: the feel of a cool refreshing shower, the anticipation of a sizzling steak on the grill, the gladness of being in touch . . .

. . . and the horror of submission.

My thoughts run together: there is no past, no present, and no future. And if there is no feeling, at least there is no pain. Unless nostalgia can hurt. Unless memories can cause suffering. Unless pure thought can evoke sorrow and heartache. Nothing can ever wound me again, except the ideation of what could have been . . .

. . . or what may be.

       *   *   *   *   *

I was guilty.

Of that there was no doubt. The evidence was so irrefutable that I wouldn't even attempt to deny it. I did what I did with little sorrow and in full consciousness. I was given no choice for one of my temperament. I was forced as irresistibly as one who steps off a cliff is drawn to the ground. I did not weigh the consequences of my actions, only the necessities.

My only regret is the failure of my mission. But given the opportunity I would try, try again.

Alone in my small cell, I awaited the verdict of sentence. There could be only one of two: life or death, with no in-between. One meant loneliness, the other meant freedom. Neither meant continuance.

A shadow flickered across the tiny square of light that suffused through the cell's translucent window: a thick, plastiglass porthole in the middle of the hermetically sealed door. The heavy portal was covered by the same padding that veneered the walls and floor and high ceiling. No chances were being taken that I might harm myself, for that pleasure was being reserved.

The door swung open on well-oiled vault hinges. Dempster Barnstall, my dapper and peach-fuzzed court-appointed attorney stepped hesitantly into the inner gloom. The door slammed behind him and by the way he looked back, you would have thought that it sealed his doom instead of mine.

He stood awkwardly and uncomfortably, one hand touching the door as if for security. He neither moved nor motioned. Not being used to the darkness of a maximum security prison cell, he squinted in my direction. I imagined that he did not truly know where I sat - or even if the cell was occupied.

But I could see him perfectly. He was dressed in the same white, universal one-piece garb that I wore - it had no pockets and no buttons and was no stronger than paper so that one could not strangle oneself with it. The material was water soluble, which prevented death by swallowing and gagging. He wore an expression that was blank except for a barely perceptible hint of fear.

Neither of us made a sound. Barnstall's eyes adjusted themselves to the dark, and I saw them narrow as they focused on mine.

"What's the verdict?" My question was a whisper, but it broke the silence like a clap of thunder. He shrank backward.

Barnstall was young: just out of law school and not yet into private practice. I didn't know how green he was, but I suspected that this might have been his first case, although he had handled it well - as well, that is, as one can handle a defendant who had already been prejudged by a rigid and unforgiving court. Despite his neophyte position, he had played a hard game, seeking, as I had instructed him, not acquittal but reduction in sentence. I could almost laugh at the irony of his losing his first case. But not quite.

He blew air into his chubby cheeks and opened his mouth to speak, but he choked on his words. That in itself was my answer. Nevertheless, he knelt before me and took one of my cold hands in his.

"The verdict is guilty," he said simply, sorrowfully. Then he swallowed, and said, "And the sentence is life."

"Oh, no," I breathed through clenched teeth. My heart sank in a turmoil of emotion as the horror was brought home in stunning reality.

"I tried, Margaret. I did all I could," pleaded Barnstall. "I argued, but they wouldn't listen. I begged for the death penalty, but it was no use. They want you - they need you. Your membership in the Cause and your acts of rebellion gave them the excuse they needed to keep you alive."

In that moment I knew despair. Where before I had faced only a nightmare, now I confronted unalterable truth. The bliss of death was denied me.

It was this kind of tyranny, this kind of indignity, that had made me join the Cause. And the irony was that I would suffer the fate against which I had fought. To not even be allowed to rest in peace . . .

I stared at Barnstall blindly, not knowing what to say. In answer, he gave my cradled hand two rapid squeezes - *the sign of the Cause!* He was one of us. The Cause had been watching over me, and yet they had been powerless to help me. My case was indeed lost.

The padded cell door popped open, knocking Barnstall out of the way. Two bulky, white-clad orderlies pounced into the tiny room. Firing from the hip, one of them shot a hypnocapsule into my face. I realized what was happening but acted too slowly. By the time the puff of white smoke had been absorbed by the air, I had already inhaled the couple of parts per billion that would induce the hypnotic reaction.

I could see and hear and feel everything that was going on around me, but I could not consciously control my motor muscles. I became a zombie, soft and pliant to the will of others, unable to resist foreign command. I was led out of the room into a white hospital corridor and placed on a gurney. I did not struggle while I was being strapped down - I *could* not struggle.

A doctor stared down at me emotionlessly. Her blonde hair was tied back in a bun with an air of professionalism. Her white gown was immaculate, her collar open, revealing a pearly patch of unblemished skin. Her bodice bulged healthily.

Urgently she ran her hands over my body, poking, prodding, and squeezing painfully. She examined my eyes, ears, nose, and throat; she listened to my heartbeat; she felt my pulse. In a faraway voice she pronounced me hearty. But her words were muffled, and I grasped her meaning more by her wave of contempt. The hypnocapsule had affected me in such a way that, although I could hear sounds, I could not distinguish intelligible language.

I wanted to scream, but neither my larynx nor my tongue nor my mouth would cooperate - I was cut off from all forms of communication. I could not furl my brow or twitch my ears or make any kind of facial expression. Only the autonomic processes continued unimpeded: breathing, swallowing, and blinking. And with great effort I could roll my eyes.

The doctor left my field of vision as the two orderlies, one on each side, set the gurney into motion. With the slight jarring movement, my head lolled to one side: I could not summon the strength to keep it upright. I had a last fleeting glimpse of Barnstall as I was accelerated on smooth, silent, rubber wheels.

He appeared lost and forlorn, like a little boy watching his mother's body being lowered into the grave. I glared back at him like an idiot.

The gurney gained speed as the two orderlies efficiently pushed it along a seemingly endless corridor. With my head rolled to one side, I concentrated my gaze on white walls and white ceiling tiles and the repetitiously spaced fluorescent lights. Hardly slowing down, the gurney swerved into another corridor, the only difference being that this one was wider and brighter than the first.

The momentum of the turn caused my head to roll to the other side as if it were an unconnected lump of flesh. I called to the orderly with my eyes, beseechingly, but he did not glance down. He stared straight ahead like a living automaton, insensitive to my discomfort and embarrassment.

We passed many doors and several cross-connecting corridors before the gurney crashed through a set of swinging double doors. I was brought to a halt in the middle of an immaculate white room that was crammed with life-support equipment: the launching pad which would insure that I did not cheat society by dying. The gruesome operation would take place without preamble.

Little time had been wasted in getting me here after the final verdict had been reached. I held the feeling that the hospital staff must have been waiting - gloating - over my fate. I would afford them another chance to practice their inhuman vivisection.

The restraining straps were unlashed and I was picked up and transferred to the operating table. Because of my lack of muscular control, my head fell back uselessly and clunked when I was set down. It was left at an awkward and uncomfortable angle until a white-smocked man came alongside and placed it on a block where it could be smeared with lather. In minutes my already short, prison style coiffure was shaved off and my bare head was daubed in antiseptic. I shivered as much from fright as from the cooling effect of the alcohol.

The barber left and was replaced by a swarm of new and emotionless attendants. Their faces were cold and businesslike. One by one, they donned featureless white cloth masks. Their eyes glowered as they prepared me like a laboratory specimen for an experiment.

My gown was stripped off and tossed aside. The white clad horde closed in like leering vampires. They stretched out my limbs and strapped them securely to the table: ankles, knees, thighs, wrists, elbows, and biceps. A metal clamp, inner lined with an absorbent pad, was fitted across my forehead and tightened until my skull was perfectly immobilized. The bottom of the band protruded below my eyebrows so that I could see it like the peak of a cap.

Wires were taped to my skin. Fine electrodes were imbedded subcutaneously. An oxygen hose was inserted into my nose and pushed down my throat. I was provided with saliva evaporators and intravenous needles and a urinary catheter. I had the feeling that I was being neatly and scientifically raped.

Able to move nothing but my eyes, I gazed anxiously around the room, assailed by the monotonous whiteness. People and objects alike seemed to melt together like whitewashed images. My only hold on reality was the erratic movement of hospital personnel. I prayed for a touch of color, even the barest hint of gray, to offset that cold, sterile environment.

My prayer was soon answered. A black face appeared in the air over the operating table. His lower face was hidden behind the inevitable bleached-white mask, but the dark eyes stared out from a frame of skin that was of the deepest ebony. I sensed concern in those murky depths.

Warm, practiced hands explored my body, massag-

ing muscles, adjusting straps, comforting an uneasy
mind. His careful handling knew softness and caring.
He loosened the head brace and fixed it into a more
comfortable position. He cloaked my nakedness with a
clean, white sheet.

He was forced back by the bustling attendants
making last minute electrical connections. But he shot
a furtive glance around the room, quickly centered his
eyes on mine, and winked. There was kindness even on
the way to the gallows.

The crowd grew larger as an assemblage of doctors
entered the room, ominous looking in their white flowing gowns and masked and hooded features. With
hands held aloft, fingers pointed upward, and wearing
sterile rubber gloves, they reminded me of a covey of
priests about to perform the rites of exorcism.

They walked around the table with stern scientific
interest, studying my head but avoiding my eyes. No
one acknowledged my presence as a person, as a
human being with rights and feelings and emotions. I
was simply a job: an operation to be carried out by
order of the court, or a number on a plastic slate that
had to be erased.

When it was all over, they would sit down and have
a cup of coffee and joke about their latest experiences
and escapades, and go out into the world and home to
their families without ever giving a thought to the inner
cruelty which they had allowed themselves to be dictat-
ed into executing. They would consider themselves
mature and civilized people who belonged to a society
that did not rely on punishment by death, for that was
a vulgarity reserved for backward cultures and jungle
tribes. Today they could praise themselves as members
of a technological society that handled criminal situa-
tions with unprejudiced callousness and rational disdain.

With these thoughts came pain. Not the pain of tor-
ture, of needles, of scalpels cutting derisively, but the
mental pain that comes with the anticipation of the
unknown.

The real pain was fear.

People can't treat others like machines, or they become machines themselves. You can't call them by numbers or stack them on shelves or put them into storage when they are unneeded. They require a special kind of maintenance called caring.

Human beings can't be raised by a mechanical nurse, taught by a computer, treated as a commodity, fed like pouring gasoline into a car. They need a semblance of belonging and the guidance of love.

It is this delicately patterned ensemble that makes mankind different from animals. It is not just the intellect but the compassion, the sentiment, and the sensitivity that makes humanity all that it is. For only people can be aware of what is in their hearts.

Like an understanding smile and the helping hand held out to a lonely child, that one wink conveyed more compassion than a lifetime of political promises.

Through this motley group of oglers, I caught sight of my black savior again. He rolled a portable life-monitoring computer to the foot of the table and began plugging in the various wires that covered my body like a loosely woven shroud. All the doctors but one moved out of my field of view as assistants handed color-coded spade lugs to the black man for terminal connection.

Meanwhile, the lone doctor inspected me. She looked different from when I had first seen her outside my cell, her bland face hidden behind a swath of gauze and her blonde bun concealed under a white skullcap. But her eyes looked the same: cold and calculating. She was female only in the physical embodiment and external sexual characteristics that were attributed to her gender. But the emotional qualities of womanhood were absent.

She finally left without a word, and I swung my gaze back to the black man attending the computer. Annunciator lights blinked off and on as he made the final connections and adjustments to the circuitry. When he nodded that everything was in working order, one of the assistants pressed a button that caused the table to fold in the middle, forcing my helpless body to a sitting position. A faint, momentary smirk was all the recognition he could give me.

Now I commanded a different view of the operating room. Where before I saw only faces and upper chests, and little of the room's perimeter, now one half of the room was invisible to me, but I could see the rest in its entirety. All the doctors and attendants were conversing inaudibly behind me. I was staring directly at the swinging double doors when they burst open, admitting to the operating room two orderlies pushing a portable life-support cubicle.

The large, plastiglass coffin-on-wheels was sealed off completely from the outside world. Oxygen was pumped in through hoses, blood and fluids were transfused through tubes, and heart pumps, lung compressors, and electronic cybernetic devices were serviced through an intricate array of double redundant electrical relays and printed circuit boards. Emergency power was supplied by the battery system in the base, which also energized the motor for self propelling. Ancillary readouts were displayed overhead.

The self-contained cubicle was designed to keep alive a person who was critically near death - or to maintain the autonomic functions of one who had clinically died and whose body was being kept in service until a replacement could be found.

I was that replacement.

The unit was plugged into the hospital power outlets, which also recharged the batteries. Most of the attendants filed out of the door, leaving the black man to oversee the cubicle's patient.

I studied the aged and decrepit occupant. She was so frail that it seemed as if a puff of wind could blow her away. Her loose skin hung in folds and was creased like crumpled paper. Her frame was light and skeletal. Her closed eyes were sunken into deep pits.

The top of her skull had been removed, exposing a wrinkled, jellied mass of gray matter. Only the pulsing of tiny veins on the top of her brain indicated that life still resided in this comatose figure. And soon this withered, useless old woman would again cherish youth and foster hope for the future. This antique patron, this valued member of state, was about to be reincarnated.

For, although brain transplants were still medically and technologically impossible, the quantum of her memory pattern was about to be transferred to a new storehouse - my own brain. But first, my mind and memory would have to be erased. The entity that was me, my soul, my personality, must first be dissociated from the physical processes of the brain in order to clear the path for its new entrant.

This was the price one paid for rebelling against establishment. This was what it was like to be a human being in a world of robots. This was the final sentence for dissension in a society which disallowed free thinking, and which did not permit an individual to stand up for what she was, or to decide for himself what he wanted - or to suggest to others that they may choose their own direction in life even if it conflicted with what the government had ordered.

It was not simply that these were dangerous thoughts, it was that *all* thoughts were dangerous. Choice was decreed by the nameless "they" who controlled the administration of state. Things were not done for the public good, but for the good of those who ruled the public. Decisions handed down by the court, itself an extension of the state, were not to be challenged or rebutted. Individuality was anathema.

Since I had no rights as a person, or even to pretend to *be* a person, I must pay for my opinions by forfeiture of the only thing I could claim as a possession. My sacrifice would be more than a life of enslavement, or release through death. My fate was the ultimate loss of freedom.

The black man conducted a thorough check of the cubicle monitors, read the latest data from my life support computer, then nodded to the doctors behind me, speaking words which, because of the hypnoinjection, were mere babble to me. It was then that I comprehended that this man was more than a technician - he was in charge. He was not a doctor, he was not performing the actual operation, but he was directing the procedure. He was in control.

The whine of a motor and the scent of ozone warned me that the laser generator had been started. It hummed a chant that would power a fine beam of destruction that could cut through everything from stainless steel to skin and bone. My eyes widened in dreadful anticipation.

I felt a warm pressure against my wrist. I looked down and saw the naked black hand, the only splash of color in the unchanging whiteness of the room and the bleached paleness of my own skin. I saw the muscles and tendons of his strong forearm flex, I saw protruding veins ripple across the back of his hand. I saw and felt his fingers clench rhythmically. With all the electronic monitoring equipment at his back, there was no reason for him to take my pulse - *he was giving me the sign of the Cause!*

My hopes soared. First Barnstall, now him. The Cause was watching over me - but how could they expect to help? We were not revolutionaries. We did not plunder and destroy and violate. We fought with ideas, as an example to the misguided masses. My position was untenable, my only salvation to become a martyr. Was this his only purpose, to grant understanding - and to say thank you for my sacrifice?

I felt a stab of pain that seared like a brand, then burrowed into my skull like a flame-thrower. Slowly, it moved around my head, dragging the pain with it. With scientific precision it knifed through scalp and skull to a depth prescribed by the laser beam's length, severing bone and tissue but leaving untouched the tender seat of intelligence.

The laser dug a narrow ditch, passing first over one ear, then above the temple, then, as a white cuff passed in front of my eyes, through my forehead, past temple and ear, and back to the point of origin. Whispering vacuum pumps sucked blood out of the incision. A small excess seeped beneath the metal clamp, ran down the bridge of my nose, and touched my lips. I tasted salt on my paralyzed tongue and smelled its wild scent above the aseptic odor of ever-present alcohol.

The hum of the laser generator whined down like a retreating honeybee that had just lapped its fill of nectar. At once I felt a great weight lifted off my head, and a curious kind of draft that quickly became icy cold.

Minutes passed during which nothing occurred. I riveted my eyes on the black man, who alternated his stare between me, the buzz of voices behind me, and the monitoring equipment. I looked vainly for some sign that this awful procedure would be interrupted - but could not imagine how it could come about.

I felt a tickling, as with a feather, on the top of my head: it was the force field of an electronic probe that was directly stimulating the cerebrum. Fine tendrils of electricity surrounded and separated nerve cells, disrupted synapses, isolated conscious processes from my memory pattern, while leaving intact the voluntary functions. What I at first perceived as pleasure grew into bitter cold, as if sharp icicles were stabbing into the gray matter, then intensified into burning pain, as from a shower of red hot sparks. In an instant it was over.

There was no more pain, no more pleasure, no more physical sensation. I seemed to float out of my body as if it were no longer part of me. And in a sense it was not, for the part of my mind that controlled it had been utterly and irrevocably severed. I had lost the sense of touch - forever.

To me, my body was an unfeeling vegetable: a limp, lifeless thing waiting for commands that would not come until a new driver had been installed. I stared in envy at the worthless, dried-up prune in the life support cubicle: the person who would soon have her neuropatterns imprinted where mine had once been.

With a jolt I realized that something else had occurred - the antiseptic odor of alcohol was gone. And with that thought, the salty taste of blood in my mouth disappeared. My brain centers were being separated one by one from their senses.

Silence reigned. I heard no more voices, no more shuffling about, no more clanking of tools, no more whishing of pumps or whine of motors. There was not even a ringing in my ears - it was as if sound had never existed. The silence was deep, ethereal, and unalterably eternal.

The corporeality of my brain would endure, but the cognitive concept of 'me' was being unquestionably pushed aside. All sensory inputs were being taken from me. Without input there could be no awareness, and without awareness there could be no identity of self.

If someone from the Cause was going to save me, help had better arrive soon, or I -

Somehow, impossibly, my point of view had shifted. Was this it? Was this the time of insurgence? Had help arrived in time?

I was doomed to disappointment, for I finally comprehended that I had not moved at all. The shift of viewpoint existed only in my sight. The difference was the loss of depth of field - I had been blinded in one eye.

My remaining seeing eye stared immovably into space. There was nothing for it to see but unholy whiteness. It could not blink, it could not move, it could not focus.

A fuzzy darkness obliterated the white panorama, surrounding two tiny, piercing orbs. Those orbs prophesied no hope, and no future. But the pearly pendant that fell from one of them shouted compassion.

Then the compassionate black face leaped into my eye and my world went dark - forever.

*   *   *   *   *

I am not dead.

Unbelievably, I have survived the operation. I have no idea how this has occurred, for I am certain that the disconnection of the memory pattern from the brain should result in the death of the psyche. There can be no life without corporeity, yet I exist.

And I think.

My death, defined as the cessation of thought, cannot occur until my physical brain ceases to function. I am kept alive because my brain is occupied by another personality which contains its own memory pattern. And I am doomed to live and to think inside a body over which I have no control, and of which I can have no awareness - and which can have no awareness of me.

But I am here, and will remain, until the end of eternity. A world without stimulus is a world without time.

At first I thought I would go crazy. Once, when I was a little girl, I locked myself in a closet. Among the toys and shoeboxes and dangling coats and dresses, I found a new world of imagination - at first fun and interesting, but then lonely and frighteningly silent. When the novelty wore off, fear set in. I cried and screamed and beat my small fists against the door. I clawed at the walls, pulled down the clothes, and beat my head on the floor. I thought I was going to die from fright. By the time my mother heard me and let me out, I was sobbing hysterically. I had been in there all of ten seconds.

Now I can't cry. Now I can't scream. Now there is no hope. And now I can't die. I am immortal and will be here until time is no more.

Am I insane? Can insanity exist if there is no way to express it?

Sometimes I think that I exist only in my imagination. I philosophize whether or not that makes sense, or whether it matters whether it makes sense. Or whether anything makes sense. I can think about it all I want because time is either infinite or it does not exist at all.

Sometimes, I even talk to myself.

Margaret, I call.

Don't be foolish, I answer. Talking to yourself is a sign of lunacy. But insanity is an abnormality, and in a world where only *I* exist, how can I be abnormal? I am I am I. I am caught in an endless circle.

My reality is bounded by memory. My expression of reality is a daydream. How can I distinguish the two? One cycles back to the other, ad infinitum . . .

Margaret, are you there?

Don't answer! Ignore it.

I remember (or dream?) that as a child I perceived things differently. I did not assume that everything I saw was righteous, or that people who spoke necessarily spoke the truth, or that life went on the way it did because it was static. I believed first in myself, then in others and in how they affected me. And lastly, in whether I wanted to be affected that way. And I believed that if things were not right, they should be changed.

But change is painful to some. Narrow minds scream when they are broadened. Why take a chance on losing what we have in order to seek something hypothetical that we may never obtain, they asked? Why should we suffer more?

Oh, they have suffered already. Yet they have not suffered enough. Why suffer at all when all that is required is change - not through violence, nor through revolution, but through evolution? Doctrines are not sacred; nor is it sacrilege to change them.

When I grew up, I found that I was not so different after all. There were others who harbored the same expressions of thought. We wanted things for ourselves: not to take away from others what they wanted, but neither to accept dictates contrary to our desires. Think and let think was the doctrine of the Cause.

Margaret, can you hear me?

Later. Let me alone. I'm dreaming.

We kept to ourselves, meeting in small groups in one another's apartments. We talked openly; we exchanged thoughts freely. We encouraged people to join us. And as if by magic, our sphere of influence increased explosively. We infected the populace like an epidemic disease. People learned that they liked to think for themselves, and to make the decisions that ruled their lives. And they wanted something back for what they put into the State.

And laws came to pass. Government became almighty. Nonconformity became criminal. And we, the leaders, became hunted.

We fought back, but we fought back with peace. We did not pillage and plunder, or rape and injure, for we wanted to create and not destroy. We merely promoted the truth: I want something for myself.

Our thinking was radical, not our doing. For that is how a civilized society progresses: not by violence, but by logic. Arguments can only be proven by reason, not by resonance.

For that I was sentenced to a living death.

But in my mind, which was all that I possessed, I continued to plot. I dreamt of the things I would have done if I had been allowed to live, and of the future of which I was no longer a part.

Margaret, are you sure you can't hear me? Or don't you want to answer me?

Part of that dream was a game I played with myself that I would someday return to the real world. I conjured up impossible circumstances in which I was reincarnated in the form of a heroine, to play out my part in the revolution of ideas.

These dreams were not wholly idle speculation, for they accorded me security and mental stability. They helped me to wile away eternity.

Margaret, please answer me.

My own answers stimulated a further response. It was almost like having a companion.

All right, I'm answering.

Can you hear me okay?

How can I hear you when I have no ears?

But you do hear me?

I am aware of you within my mind. But it's impossible for me to hear you.

You're right, of course. You don't strictly hear me. We call it musing.

I find nothing funny about it.

Musing, not amusing. You need ears to hear, but you can muse with your mind.

Is that what I'm doing right now?

Yes. I've been trying to muse you for a long time.

I never heard you before. Er, that is, I never mused

you before.

That's because you weren't ready yet.

Weren't ready for what?

For musing.

Why?

Musing is a sensitivity of which normal people are unaware.

Then how can I be aware of it? Are you suggesting that I'm not normal?

Yes, I am. You're not normal - at least, not any more. You've been cut off from all physical sensory inputs.

I know that.

Well, the brain, like any other organ or part of the body, compensates for injuries by making itself stronger in other ways. It's part of the healing process. In the case of a permanently injured arm, the other arm must take on more of a burden and the resulting exercise strengthens it. Likewise, a brain separated from its tactile stimulations learns to utilize mental skills which are normally subdued. That is to say, the ability to muse is usually overpowered by the magnitude of impressions received through the five physical senses that we know as sight, hearing, touch, taste, and smell. Your sensitivity to the sixth sense is dulled by the input from the other five. This situation almost never comes about because in most cases brain death is the natural result of stimulus cessation - meaning, the cessation of all the bodily functions. Your body, however, is not dead. It is being kept alive by another memory pattern that has been superimposed on your brain's storage cells. Another identity now controls your body, thus releasing the hidden potential of your mind.

There is logic to your argument, but it all sounds so mystical.

That's a very coincidental word choice, for mystics have long been known to possess powers beyond accepted understanding. Call them mediums, or occultists, or, in ridicule, fakers and illusionists: they are people who have and who can demonstrate an unusual sensitivity toward mental perceptions and abilities. Usu-

ally by putting themselves in a trance - a state of mind which represses normal inputs - they can evoke the subliminal powers of the brain. This leads to all forms of manifestations of paranormal or psychic talents.

I still don't know whether to believe you.

But you must admit that you muse me.

I admit only that I have conjured up some kind of psychological barrier that makes my confinement bearable and which helps to ward off insanity.

Then how do you perceive me?

I'm not certain that I perceive you at all. You may be nothing more than a figment of my imagination. This musing you talk about, or muse about, just doesn't make any sense.

But it is the very quintessence of sense: not in a physical context, but as the product of pure thought.

By that definition you don't exist because you, yourself, are a product of that pure thought.

No, I exist because I'm a different entity of thought. We can communicate through musing but we have separate physical locations. You are you, and I am I.

And never the twain shall meet.

But we can communicate.

Or I can talk to myself - the effect is the same. One is no better than the other.

Except that I can help you to discover your latent talents. You must do that much for yourself, if not for us.

Us?

I am not alone. There are others.

And who are they?

They are other members of the Cause who have preceded you into oblivion.

Why can't I muse them?

Because, like a child who can hear but does not understand the language, you cannot interpret their muses. And also, like a child who speaks baby talk, you are very difficult to understand. But I, like a parent, have been with you since the beginning, and can distinguish your disconnected muses.

Will I ever be able to muse them?

Not only will you, but you must. We need you. The Cause needs you. All of humanity needs you.

You're musing in riddles.

I'm sorry. I guess I should explain. But I've had such a difficult time getting you to believe in me *that I doubt that you'd believe the rest of it.*

I've got the time to listen if you've got the time to muse.

Very well. In that case I have good news for you. Eventually you will be able to push aside the imprinted memories of your intruding identity, and regain control of your body.

Now I know I'm dreaming.

It's true. Your mind is your own, and it can never be subjugated to the will of another. Even as we muse, your brain is healing: regenerating its neural pattern, rebridging broken synapses, mending lesions. Soon you will be able to see the blue ocean, hear the crashing of waves upon the sandy beach, taste and smell the salt air, bask in the warmth of the sun, shiver in the chill of the water, and feel the crunch of shells underfoot. But all these things will be secondary to the new powers and abilities that will have been freed. You will be reborn a new woman in your own body.

You fill me with such hope that I want to believe you. I need to believe you. But what will happen to the old woman who has been given control of my body? Where will she go?

She will earn the fate which was intended for you. Her mind does not have the intimate knowledge of the bypaths of your brain that you have. In a manner of speaking, your brain waves will be able to outrun hers, so that your thoughts will always arrive first. You can outthink her at every turn, giving you complete physical control. She will still exist, but only ephemerally. She will be locked in an ironic prison, able to see and hear and feel, but not to motivate. You will be in charge. Then you can help us.

How?

You will be the perfect spy. To the world, you will

have a new identity, that of Division Overlord Rachel Cumberland. Her every memory will be at your command so you can imitate her personality, but you will govern her actions. And you will continue to fight for the Cause, and for the freedom of the people.

You make it sound so great.

Believe me, Margaret. Believe in me, Margaret. It will happen.

Oh, I do believe you. I need you so. Please don't leave me.

I'll always be within musing distance.

Thank you. I feel very close to you.

You are very close to me - closer than you think. I'll be watching over you. And if you ever need me, I will always be here to wink at you - again.

Then I mused his face and wonderfully dark eyes, and imagined a gathering tear. And mentally, in inner glee, I shed a tear myself.

"How do you feel today, Rachel?" he asked, putting the stethoscope up to his ears with strong, ebony hands.

"Very well, Dr. Philmont," she said, jumping slightly as the cold diaphragm touched her bare chest. "I feel distinctly uncoordinated, but I managed to walk around a little. It's great to be back in a youthful body again. I'm quite proud of this one."

Dr. Philmont smiled, and said, "I want you to take better care of yourself than you did before. That means no smoking, a good diet, and daily exercise. You take care of your body and your body will take care of you."

Dr. Philmont shrugged off the stethoscope and tucked the diaphragm into an open shirt pocket. Glancing at his watch, he picked up her wrist and, with practiced fingers, felt her pulse.

"This body responds well in other ways, too, Doctor," said Rachel, blinking coyly. She reached across with her other hand and ran it along Dr. Philmont's thigh. "I can't wait to try it out. Are you going to continue to examine my control response?"

"Certainly. I'll keep you under strict medical observation."

"Why don't you come back this evening with your rubber mallet and other tools and test my reflexes again? I think they're definitely improving."

"Well, I don't know. I have other rounds to make."

"You can't work all the time. And anyway, I'm a very important patient. I'll need special attention. I'll have a bottle of wine and a couple glasses sent up with dinner, and we can talk about some of the nonmedical aspects of my recovery. After that we can . . . "

Rachel choked on her words. She grabbed a tissue from the nightstand and dabbed her eyes.

"Is anything wrong?" asked Dr. Philmont.

"I - I don't know. I felt fine, then all of a sudden, I had an urge to cry. I don't know what I could have been thinking."

Dr. Philmont held the side of her face for a moment and peered into her eyes. "Nothing to worry about," he said at last. "It's a temporary loss of control reaction. It's quite normal."

"Thank you. I'm not really worried at all," Rachel said, cupping his hand to her face. "Not as long as you're around."

Dr. Philmont pulled away, and said, "Perhaps I *will* stop around tonight."

"I'll order the wine."

At the door, Dr. Philmont stopped, turned around, and winked.

Rachel's hand, of its own accord, waved back. She did not know it yet, but she was about to experience the supreme form of quadriplegia - including the loss of all five senses - for the rest of her unendurable life.

When Love Has Gone

I never would have let her in if it hadn't been raining so hard. I don't even like dogs, especially a German shepherd the size of a small horse. They are loud and rough and can eat you out of house and home. And what they don't knock over in their blundering gait they cover with globs of thick hair, unless they are combed religiously. Besides that, I was out here for solitude. If I wanted to burden myself with company, I could only be tempted by a smooth-skinned creature with a pretty smile and a warm, soft body. Someone, say, like Alice.

But Alice was dead, and there was no getting away from it. A wife and a life-long companion cannot be resurrected in the form of a dog.

For a moment I was lost in nostalgic memories of a vibrant woman, full of love and compassion and the indomitable faith of youth. I raw the red-lipped smile and the wind-swept curls and the dancing blue eyes. But she was nothing more than a phantom - one that was visible but not quite solid.

A fierce bolt of lightning leaped into the clouds from a tall dune on the other side of the salty, shallow bay, and was followed by a peal of thunder that jarred me off my feet. I was startled by its abruptness for an instant. My hackles rose in deference to the discordant clap.

That silent, canine visage redirected my attention. The dog, at least, had not been frightened by the electric display. But the eyes had come alive with a ferocious craving. The once-weary, half-drowned dog seemed to have gained strength. I, on the other hand, felt momentarily weak, as if all my energy had been drained like a capacitor put to ground.

Imagination can be a blessing or a curse, depending upon whether it is in control or not.

In the dim tungsten light, I stared unhappily at the dog on the doorstep. With haunting familiarity it stared back - with dark, importuning eyes, shivering ever so slightly for extra effect. I knew then that I had been caught on the rebound. Having lost Alice so recently, my sympathy level was at ebb. Shaking my head and pursing my lips in resignation, I stepped aside and made a grand bow and sweeping arm gesture that invited the animal inside.

I shut the door and watched in astonishment as the German shepherd waddled to the far corner of the one-room cabin and lay down on a pile of loose rags. I saw then that she was a bitch, and a big one at that. Without the several gallons of water that matted down her two-tone hair, she must have tipped the scales at ninety pounds.

In slippered feet, I shuffled to the corner that served as a kitchen. There was nothing more to it than an antique refrigerator, an electric range, and a cracked porcelain sink. Food and dishware were all arrayed on open shelving

I plopped down in a rickety chair and leaned my elbows wearily on the tiny bench-that-served-as-a-table. In front of me was a cup of coffee that had been rapidly cooling while I had been holding a silent conversation with a dumb dog. The coffee was ice cold, as if it had been sitting there for an hour instead of five minutes. But once the liquid touched my lips, I couldn't resist it, and drank it right down.

I knew then that it would not be enough. I put a pot of water on the range and started looking for something to eat. I pulled down a loaf of bread, ripped open the cellophane, and crammed a fistful of it into my mouth. While chewing, I opened the refrigerator door and scooped out whatever I could find. In short order I demolished three uncooked hotdogs, a bowl of cold soup, a baked potato leftover from last night's supper, a small jar of mayonnaise (which I scooped out with a spoon), and a dish of pudding. And this was before the water boiled!

I fixed my instant coffee and while it cooled, I opened a can of soup and drank it straight from the can without ever checking to see what kind it was. Then I sipped my coffee and contemplated the mysterious dog.

The bedraggled bitch was curled up with eyes closed in apparent unconcern, her scratched snout resting on white paws. With a flash of insight, I realized that I had seen this dog before - that is, a picture of her. In my mind, I flew back to that day when, drunk with despair, I had ventured through the wooded marshland searching for this very cabin.

The Virginia that I had always pictured was one of colorful mountains and broad meadows and an endless patchwork quilt of textured farmland; of deciduous forests harboring white-tailed deer, fox and bobcat, vultures and ravens and a variety of warblers; of deep clear lakes surrounded by grasslands of shrubs and violets and wild orchids. But this marshy peninsula that separated the blue Atlantic from the muddy Chesapeake offered a beauty and splendor all its own.

From the highway I had seen perfectly plowed fields in which were grown luxuriant soy beans, plump watermelons, and yellow-tasseled corn: now tilled under since early fall. But once off the smooth macadam, the dreamy, rural, shoulderless roads sliced through thick groves of cedar, pine, and leafless oak abound with hyperactive chipmunks and chattering squirrels. As I neared the eastern wetlands, the trees thinned out as cedar streams merged with salt marshes giving rise to woodbine and marsh grass. The migratory Canada geese were gone but the bay area remained a year-round refuge for ducks, gulls, and herons.

With the realtor's hand-drawn map braced on the steering wheel, I tried hard to keep the rattling jeep on the dirt trail. Coming to a fork, I veered left and kept going for what seemed like miles before I came to a clearing with a tin shack bounded on one side by pine trees and on the other by salt swamp.

It was already starting to drizzle, so I hardly noticed

the sagging roof or the peeling sides. It had been hot and sunny when I had left town and I was quickly chilling down in the cold front of the forthcoming storm. My long-johns and flannels were packed away under the canvas tarp in the back seat, along with several months of provisions and five-gallon cans of gasoline for the generator. Open military jeeps bestowed manly appeal, but ninety percent of the time they were too damned impractical. Like now.

I charged into the shack cursing the agent who had duped me with visions of a winter chalet. I jumped back in surprise when I saw the back of an old man stoking timber into an ancient wood-burning stove. He turned around slowly and without surprise.

I didn't know whether to feel embarrassment or anger, while mentally I located the rental agreement.

"Didn't know there was company coming," said the man in a creaky but sonorous voice, "but as long as you're here, make yourself at home."

"Uh, well, I'm . . . That is, I'm looking for a cabin . . . unoccupied of course . . ." My voice trailed off as I took notice of my surroundings. What I at first took to be a shambles actually seemed to be rather orderly. It's just that without closets and cabinets, all the things that were usually hidden from view were in the open. But they were placed neatly, in an order that probably suited the old man's lifestyle. "And it's supposed to have electric heat, refrigerator and range, storm windows, antenna, and," I hesitated slightly in my brochure monologue, "a bay view."

"Sounds like the Bleiler place, 'bout three mile down the road. Heard tell his daughter was selling out."

"Three more miles!" I exclaimed. "I didn't know it was that far out."

"Old Bleiler, he loved the wilderness, shootin' duck and trappin' coon, as if he couldn't afford to buy decent food. That what you looking for?"

"Well, I'm only renting it - with an option to buy," I explained.

My host finished stuffing wood into the stove and

slammed the iron door shut with a clang. When he stood up, I was forced to take notice of him, for he towered over my six-foot frame by at least three inches. He was as broad as an ox and weighed far on the other side of two hundred pounds. His dark hair crowned a squarish head that sported a grizzled face with a perpetual five-day beard. His flannel shirt sleeves were rolled up to the elbows, his dungarees too short even with high hunting boots.

"What you planning to do out there all by yourself?" he asked, filling a kettle from a jug and setting it on the now-roaring stove. The heat was already chasing away the goose bumps on my arms. "City folk don't usually like it out here in the winter. The weather can get real nasty at times. And there ain't much to do without a phone or TV."

"I brought a portable with me, and a lot of books. I can do without a phone for a while."

"Running away from something, huhn?" he asked easily.

"Well, uh, I'm not really . . ." I parried.

"That's all right, partner. I can see you don't want to talk about it. I'm out here for the solitude my own self."

I didn't know how to reply, but the old codger sensed my embarrassment.

"Hey, there's no sense standing there by the door. You may as well lay up till this storm passes." I listened to the methodical pinging of raindrops on the tin roof. In the background I heard the rumble of thunder. He put two wooden chairs in front of the stove, and said, "And as long as you're going to stay, you might as well set and have a coffee."

"That's awfully nice of you but . . ."

"No buts about it, mister. I'll get the fixin's and you get comfortable. Only don't stare at that kettle or it'll never boil."

I don't claim to be very rugged, so at that moment, nothing could have sounded better than a fireside seat and a hot cup of coffee. I sat down.

"My name's Charlie Hay. What's your'n'?"

"Dan," I said. Then, clearing my throat, "Dan Wilson."

The rain was beating down now with the roar of a subway train in a narrow tunnel. The storm-swept sky brightened intermittently as lightning lashes added to the light of a kerosene lantern hanging above the stove.

Charlie came back with a metal tray on which were two cups, two shot glasses, and a bottle of brandy.

"You wouldn't let an old man down by refusin' to drink with him, would you now?"

"You don't have to twist my arm," I said, as he filled the glasses with golden liquid and handed one to me.

"Cheers," he said. We both downed our drinks, and he poured another.

"Do you live out here by yourself?" I asked conversationally.

"Yep." He reached for the kettle and poured boiling water into the cups. When he put the kettle back on the stove, he continued, "Gets pretty lonely 'round here since old Bertha went her way," he said wistfully.

"How long has your wife been dead?" I asked.

"Nigh on fifteen year." When he saw the startled look on my face, he laughed, revealing clean, white teeth and the unmistakable signs of upper and lower plates. "Bertha's my dog. She was gettin' old so I knew she'd be a goin' soon. Been lonesome without her."

Charlie Hay fumbled with his worn, leather wallet, "Got a pixture of her here." Out came a faded black and white print, cracked with age. He passed it over. "Course, she was only a year old when that was taken. Right after the little woman passed away. Got in a fight with a cat, too, you can tell by the scratches on her nose. Those white paws she got from her maw. Don't rightly know who her paw was."

"Looks like a big dog," I said.

"Most ninety pounds, but gentle as a lamb, she was. Never hurt a soul."

"Then how'd she get in a fight with a cat?"

"Thought cats was friends and tried to nuzzle it.

Never did it again."

I laughed, and passed back the photo. "Do much hunting?" I asked, taking into account the wooden decoys and a double-barreled shotgun.

"Usta. Don't any more. Now I just carve. Besides, old Bertha could never get 'em when I did shoot 'em."

"Why not get a retriever." I suggested.

"Dogs ain't like cars. You don't trade 'em in fer new models."

Plain people and simple language often produced deep thoughts. I sipped my coffee. After a few more brandies, I really began to warm up. By the time the storm moved out to sea, it was nearly dark, so I used it as an excuse to get on my way.

Charlie and I slogged over the wet ground. When we got to the jeep, I dried off the seat as best I could, then climbed in. I pulled out the map and he ran his finger along the penciled route.

"You just follow this road out three, maybe four mile. You cross a washout just about here, then keep your eyes left until - "

He was cut off by a tremendous crack of thunder that seemed to shake the very ground. We both looked eastward, where the storm was moving off the coast. An unbelievably bright ball of light floated down from the black clouds, fluttering like a leaf in a breeze. It hit the water this side of the barrier dunes, in the narrow part of the bay on which the Bleiler cabin was situated. It hissed like a seething cauldron when it touched the cold ocean spray, and steam exploded skyward.

"Hot damn," shouted Charlie Hay. "Ball lightning. Can you beat that?"

A dark cloud of mist was all that was left of the dazzling display, but shivers ran along my body like an electric shock.

"I thought ball lightning had been largely disproved," I said.

There was nothing left now to show that the strange phenomenon had occurred.

"Don't you believe your eyes? If they ever put windows in them laboratories, them highfalutin perfessors would be able to see the real world."

I didn't comment on Charlie's homespun philosophy. I cranked up the jeep and put-putted on my way, waving to a man who had a more realistic hold on life than most people I knew - myself included.

Now, a month later, sitting cozily in my warm cabin, listening to the light drumming of rain on the shingled, A-framed roof, I saw the same dog that was in Charlie's picture. As if she did not have a care in the world, as if she weren't wet or cold or hungry, she slept peacefully.

And then in the next instant, an awful thought occurred to me: *This dog was supposed to be dead!*

A cold chill ran up and down my spine. The cup slipped out of my hand and crashed into the saucer, breaking both and spilling lukewarm coffee across the table and onto my lap. But I hardly noticed, for I was staring at the German shepherd.

And she was staring back!

Her dark eyes seemed to burn right through me. If I had been scared before, I was terrified now.

Neither of us batted an eyelash. The bitch's eyes were wide and unblinking. After what must have been several minutes, she lowered her head, closed her eyes, and went back to sleep.

I could have sworn that there was something supernatural in the room, for the air seemed to bristle. I finally made myself believe that my perception was to blame. The dog had only looked up after the crash of the cup. And when I thought about it, Charlie Hay had never said that the dog was dead. He had used euphemisms that I had interpreted to mean death. And here Bertha had been wandering in the wild all these weeks.

I hadn't seen Charlie since that day, nor ever started up the jeep. But tomorrow, I must tell him the good news. Finally, I had something to be happy about.

I went to bed in high reverie, dreaming of Alice and the days when our love was young and fresh, and the world was ours for the asking. And how much I wanted that world back again. And how impossible I knew it all was.

In the morning I was simply ravenous. I sliced thick strips off a side of bacon and let it smolder in the frying pan. I cut up two potatoes and made home fries in the grease. I had been out of fresh eggs for weeks, but there was plenty of mix. I added water to the powder and stirred it to a gluey consistency. Then I scraped out the bacon and potatoes and poured in the egg mixture. In no time at all I had a feast fit for a king.

It wasn't until I was halfway through my second cup of coffee that I paused to wonder at my newfound tranquility. Then I noticed the hairy bundle lying in the corner.

She peered up at me through half-closed eyes when I knelt down to touch her. She was in ragged condition but seemed to be suffering neither pain nor discomfort. She stretched and rolled over on her hack and tempted me to pet her. Seen like that, she was abnormally long.

Speaking in baby talk, I gave her a few gentle pats and rubbed her exposed abdomen. Then I saw evidence of her exposure to the elements, for her hair was dropping out by the handful.

Now, if there is one thing I can't stand, it is a shedding dog. But this was not natural shedding. She trembled slightly under my hand, as if in fever. And although I may not be crazy about dogs, I'm as sympathetic as the next man. I knew that she should not be moved under these circumstances, so I tried to make her as comfortable as possible.

I brought her a bowl of water and a slab of bacon, but she would touch neither. I tried to cover her quaking body, but she refused the blanket, kicking it off as soon as I placed it over her. So I lifted her up and tucked the blanket under the rags, giving her insulation as well as a softer bed.

She stared at me constantly with large, doleful eyes, and seemed to take sustenance from my commiseration. Gladly would I offer compassion, since it cost so little to give, if it would nurture this creature to health.

A sense of humanity and the possibility of future companionship would be requital enough.

I spent the morning lost in thought. The television remained unused, my books unopened. I had decided not to call on Charlie Hay until I was sure that Bertha was going to survive. After a month of mourning, it would be no relief to him to have his dog returned only to have her taken away again.

Before I knew it, lunchtime had rolled around and I was famished. I ate double portions from what I had been used to eating. And I was delighted at my restored appetite. I seemed to have discovered a new inner strength.

Bertha, however, would neither eat nor drink, and refused strongly my attempt at forced feeding. And even though I knew that she had lived surprisingly well in the wilderness, I thought that she was near death. I continued to play nurse, contributing to her health the only things that she would accept: love and pity.

Outside the cabin, darkness hung like a shroud. The afternoon had flashed by so quickly that I must have dozed off, for I remembered none of it. I approached Bertha despondently. She looked a sad sight. She was almost completely bald, great tufts of hair lying about her as if it had been shorn off with electric clippers. Only her head and lower abdomen retained any hirsute adornment. Her skin was pink and pliable, and seemed to be sagging downward. She lay almost flat on her back, a difficult position for dogs because of the protruding spine. But as always, her eyes were bright and hopeful, and followed me with intensity.

I slept peacefully again that night after a voluminous supper. I dreamt pleasant dreams of the Alice I used to know.

By morning, Bertha was in a sad state. Overnight she seemed to have become flaccid, as if she were melting into a puddle. Lying on her back, her barrel chest had flattened and spread out. Her paws no longer bent downward in a begging position, but lay beside her pink body. Her legs stretched out and had the appearance of straightness, as if the joints were dissolving. Even her tapered snout had sunk back into her face, while her head flowed into an oval, uncanine shape. But the most startlingly visible change was the alteration of her skin. Where before she had the appearance of a plucked chicken ready for roasting, now the pores had smoothed over and the skin became silky and pleasant to the touch. The only hair remaining capped the misshapen head and clung to the lower pelvis between the junction of the legs.

How long this amazing transformation would go on before she succumbed to inevitable death, I could only guess. Mercifully, I hoped it was short.

I watched her throughout the day, as I alternately devoured cans of food and dozed unaccountably. Darkness was upon me without knowledge of the passing day. I struggled for one last look at the changeling before dragging myself to bed for the night.

What I now saw lying on the blanket was astonishing, yet I accepted the transformation with equanimity. The rib cage had broadened and flattened. The forepaws lay naturally on the floor, linked to the shoulder by a parallel clavicle. The entire pelvis had rearranged itself so that the hind legs were aligned with the torso. The claws had receded into tiny nails, the digits had become manipulable, especially those of the - hands? The external labia were covered by a wiry tuft of hair resembling the mons, and of the two parallel rows of nipples, only the uppermost pair remained, bulging outward on soft pallets of flesh.

Despite the food I had consumed, I felt weak. I collapsed into bed without changing into my pajamas. Bertha's permutation seemed to be taking as much from me as a hard day's work. I lay in bed like a corpse.

Sometime during the night I heard a rustling in the cabin. I uncoiled my body and propped myself up on my elbows. Squinting through sleep-filled eyes, I saw something glimmer in the silvery moonlight. I recognized, through the mist of memory, flake-blue eyes.

She stepped lightly into the full light of the room, one side of her nude body limned sensuously. Her face was thin and delicate, her skin smooth and marmoreal. Her long neck led to strong, upright shoulders. Her breasts were small and shapely, rouged with nipples that stood out like red gumdrops. She moved sybaritically, the pretty patch of pubic hair bristling with each step.

I was captivated by her eyes as she looked down at me. I hardly dared to move. A lewd half-smile formed on her lips. She tilted her head to one side, tenderly. Her hands ran through my tangled hair, cradled my neck, and eased my head down onto the crumpled pillow. Long flowing silky hair fell off her marbled shoulders and brushed my face. Her lips touched mine, found my nose, my eyes, my neck, and then caressed my body.

I stiffened at each velvety touch. My heart and soul poured forth pent-up love. Her eyes drank it in, savoring each pulse of emotion. And I gave all I had until there was nothing left to give. I fell back exhausted and limp, to sleep the sleep of happy angels.

My life became a dream world. Alice cherished me like a pampered pet. She fed me masses of food, petted and played with me, rubbed my temples and scratched my back and massaged my feet. I hadn't felt love like this since we had first met, decades ago. I lost all track of time: my watch stopped and I forgot to check off the calendar. Day and night merged, sometimes passing like the flicker of an eye. I lived in a blind world of consuming love, knowing not where I was going, nor caring. Life faded effortlessly.

Days, perhaps weeks, later the lights flickered, and I knew that I was going to have to leave the warmth and security of the cabin to check the generator.

When I stepped into the wet snow, it was like a splash in the face. The crispness of the winter air cleared my head, and while I poured gasoline into the generator's fuel reservoir, reality seemed to descend upon me like a pall. My existence seemed morbid.

I felt hollow, as if the constant outpouring of emotion had drained my vital essence. No matter how much I loved, no matter how much I gave, I got nothing in return. I became overwhelmed with a desire for real companionship, one with positive feedback.

It was time to call on Charlie Hay.

Wearily, I hauled myself to the jeep. The stinging cold helped to keep me aware of my senses, lest delusion conquer my mind. The marshland was majestic in its white blanket: cedar branches hung heavy with snow. The air was alive with the sights and sounds of genuine being.

Charlie's door was unlocked - indeed, did not have a lock. It swung open rustily. Cold poured out as if from a freezer - the fire had long been damped. In the gloom I located the kerosene lantern and, fumbling with matches, coaxed it into service. It did little to dispel the darkness, like a lonely candle on an infinite beach.

The one-room shack was dreary and unkempt. The sink was a receptacle of unwashed dishes. Empty cans were piled high in a corner. Soiled clothing was draped on overturned furniture. Torn books and loose papers lay strewn like fallen leaves. The stench of urine and defecation and decay was heavy in the air.

A heap of ragged blankets concealed a figure on the cot. With a quaking hand I parted the rumpled covers. Charlie Hay must have been dead for weeks, but his body could have been that of a three-thousand-year-old mummy. The once tall, proud backwoodsman was now a shriveled, shrunken husk, cast aside like last year's crop. I thought of ancient parchment, or paper that had been wrinkled and crushed and allowed to unfold. His dry, brittle skin was a tawny veil over an emaciated, skeletal frame.

One gnarled hand clutched the faded portrait of Bertha, a young dog with a freshly-scratched nose, as Charlie always remembered her. It was also a portrait of the Bertha, once bitch, now woman, that had wandered onto my doorstep one stormy evening eons ago. The Bertha of today was the Bertha of Charlie's past, because that was how he kept her alive in his dreams.

More steady now, more assured, I lifted eyelids that were as delicate as burned tissue paper - and looked into emptiness. None of the depth, none of the feeling, none of the vivacity that had been Charlie Hay remained. It had all been sucked out of him as nourishment, as one sucks juice from an orange.

I stumbled away from Charlie and the truth that he portended. I leaned against the cluttered sink and peered into a dilapidated mirror. What peered out, in the weak, yellow glow of the lantern, was a dirty, bearded, haggard ghoul.

The thing that I called Alice was keeping me alive like fodder, consuming my love, eroding my humanity bit by bit, until nothing was left but an empty shell. Almost.

I tore the shotgun off its rack and stuffed half a dozen cartridges in my pocket. Hatred boiled within me and kept me warm during the ride back to my cabin.

The jeep skidded on the snow in front of the Bleiler place. I held the gun alongside my leg, away from the windows. I did not know what *it* was capable of.

It sat up on the bed as I entered, a frozen half-smile disguising sinister intent. Hands beckoned sensuously, hypnotizingly. It rose with flowing grace. Fathomless eyes searched mine, seeking the life-giving force of emotion. I poured hate into the vessel that had already stripped me of love. It could not tell the difference.

I waited until it was right in front of me before I raised the deadly twin barrels to waist level. Cold, blue eyes clashed with mine, feeding on hatred, gorging itself on self-indulgent lust, growing stronger on my passion even as I pulled the triggers and tore two gaping holes in its breast.

The force of the blast catapulted the thing against the wall, where it slithered to the floor. Unbelievably, unblinkingly, it climbed to its feet and staggered toward me. Globs of flesh were splattered on the wooden panels, and were visible through the gaping cavities. Spongy pulp fell from the wounds. Still it came closer, feeding.

I chambered two more cartridges as I backed away in panic. The gun roared in my hands and a close group of steel pellets shredded the lower abdomen. It kept coming. I loosed another shot, lower this time, severing one leg at the knee. It fell. But it crawled.

I tripped over a chair and went down with a thud. I screamed when the wall touched my shoulder, cutting off further retreat.

Powerful arms pulled what was left of the body across the floor. Scraps of flesh, hanging in tatters, were scraped off as it slithered like a wounded snake. The head stayed erect; beady eyes feasted on my fear.

It would not die. It had no vital organs; it had no heart. I could not kill it as long as it had me for sustenance. I could only sever the means of its gathering.

I shoved in the last two cartridges. It had crept up to my feet, was reaching out for me. I aimed the gun at one mesmeric orb, and fired.

Half the head came apart in a cloud of metal and mush. A thick, creamy fluid gurgled out effusively. Still it fed with one gluttonous eye.

I jammed the other barrel into that Cyclopean orb, driving hate and steel with a twitch of the finger. When the deafening roar died out, the thing lay immobile. The head looked like a smashed watermelon.

I climbed to my feet and lurched out the door. I fetched two gerry cans from the generator shed and spilled gasoline all over the cabin. Then, only one match was required to destroy every vestige of the repulsive thing.

The dry building burst into a huge orange ball, fanned by an offshore breeze. I watched ecstatically as flames leaped thirty feet into the air, accompanied by the whooshing sound of sucked-in oxygen and the crackling of disintegrating wood.

Later, when there was nothing left but a slag heap, I stirred the smoldering cinders. And later, with nightfall approaching, a whining engine stirred through the nearby woods. A four-wheel-drive pickup trampled the snowy lane and screeched to a halt by my jeep.

"Dan," shouted a husky voice. Bryan Brooks, lawyer and friend, climbed out of the cab, "My god, what happened? Are you all right?"

Listlessly I said, "I'm fine."

"You look terrible. Are you sure you're okay?"

"I'm all right, Bryan. I wasn't inside when the fire started. I'm okay. Really." It took several moments before I questioned the incongruity of his presence. "But what are you doing here?"

"It's your wife, Dan. She came back. She wants you to come home. She said she needs you."

I laughed sardonically. "Thanks, Bryan, but I won't be going back to her - ever."

"But she said she's sorry. She left that other guy. This time she says she's back for good."

"Just like she said the time before that. And the time before that. She's almost squeezed me dry. I won't let her take any more of me."

"Dan, you're not making sense.

"Face it, Bryan. She's dead.

"What do you mean, she's dead?"

"To me, she's dead. The Alice I knew died a long time ago. I just failed to realize it - or to accept it. What exists in her body now is not the woman I married. I know that now. And this time I won't forget it."

Bryan looked startled for a moment. Then gradually, a wide grin of understanding spread across his tanned face.

"Welcome back to reality," he said.

He would never know how true that statement was.

The Dimensions of Love

George Halstead forced all thoughts of the warp generator out of his mind.

"No, George, I will not go skiing with you this weekend."

Betty made it sound as if there was no question in her mind: it was an absolute. But Halstead was not beaten yet.

"Why won't you at least give it a try? You're good on water skis. There's no reason you can't learn to downhill, if only you'll give it a chance."

"I told you before: I hate cold, I hate snow, and I hate being bundled up in those color-coordinated Eskimo suits. I have a good body and I enjoy showing it off. And I wish you enjoyed looking at it as much as you enjoy lying on it."

"I do enjoy lying - looking at it."

"Then why didn't you come to the beach with me last weekend?"

That was one of the problems of living in Sacramento: it was equidistant between the ski slopes and the Pacific Ocean. A two-hour drive in either direction presented a choice of prerogatives. And Halstead, like most men, had his. "I explained that to you. You know I couldn't get away from work."

Betty dabbed rouge on her face and snapped her compact shut. "What do you mean? You're a salaried teacher with only four classes a week."

"I'm a full professor, with half a dozen ongoing research projects. And one of them happens to be very important to me."

"Yes, I know. You're so busy playing around with your test tubes and chemicals that you don't have time for any serious human involvement."

"Betty, I've told you time after time. I'm a physicist, not a chemist."

"You're a scientist and you're married to your work."

"That's not true. You know I always find time to take you to dinner."

"Twice a month does not constitute 'always.' And I want to go to places other than your apartment."

"All right, then where else would you like to go?"

"To the beach, to watch the sunset. It's so romantic."

"But you don't know the pressure I'm under. I don't have time to watch sunsets. I'm close to a big breakthrough. The mathematical construct for my interdimensional transfer is almost perfected. I've just got to work a few bugs out of the system."

"Then how come you have time to go skiing, but not to the beach?"

"I have time because my equations are being loaded into the computer and the calculations won't be done for a couple days. And in the mean time, I need some physical activity to, well, to spark my mind. Look, I sit around all day . . . "

"And most nights."

" . . . in a laboratory . . . "

"With that buxom female assistant."

" . . . punching a keyboard. By the end of the week I'm mentally exhausted. I need to get out in the fresh air, clear my thoughts, put my body to work, stretch out the old muscles. I need some physical activity."

"But the only activity you want is bedtime."

"Betty, that's not fair. I have no more than a normal sexual appetite for anyone my age - except you."

Betty jumped up off the park bench in a huff. "That's the trouble with meeting people at parties. And I know why they're called 'cocktail' parties: because the people who go to them are looking for one or the other."

Halstead grabbed her arm before she got away. "Hey, I'm willing to give this thing a chance, maybe make it permanent. But I can't do it all myself. I need some help."

"What you need is someone else. Like that luscious secretary of yours, sitting there all day long polishing her nails. George, you know what the trouble with you is? You're in love with yourself. You want a woman to do exactly what you want, whenever you want it. Well, that's just not the way this world is made. People are different, and that's what makes them interesting."

Halstead's voice crescendoed. "You're only saying that because I'm interested in my work, and you have no interests other than being wined, dined, and chauffeured about like some pampered pet."

Betty humphed, and started clicking her high heels along the tree-lined sidewalk. This did not stop her from talking, however. "If that's what you want to think, then go right ahead. But I need to be more in someone's life than an evening's entertainment, more important than a silly job."

Halstead ran to catch up with her. "This is a career, not just a job. My work is highly sophisticated research into the nature of the space-time continuum, divergent realities, and alternating time streams. All right, I have been busy lately. But that doesn't mean that there's no time for us in the future."

Betty reached her car and grasped the door handle carefully, so as not to chip her long, polished nails. "George, you're not in any reality, divergent or otherwise. And your main interest in time is in making it. I'm not going to be one of your experiments."

"Now, Betty, you're getting yourself worked up again."

"I'm also getting myself worked out. So, why don't you go find a girl who likes laboratories and ski slopes, and let me find a man who's willing to give me the time I deserve? I think we'd better end this relationship before one of us gets hurt."

She slammed the car door behind her and drove away.

*   *   *   *   *

Halstead unbuttoned his white smock and pulled a worn leather wallet out of his pocket. "Barbara, I've got twenty dollars here that says you're not doing anything this weekend."

Barbara smiled over the keys of her electric typewriter. "You're right. But if I agreed to go skiing with you, you'd lose the bet."

"How did you know that I was going skiing?"

She pointed out the window with a manicured hand. "The racks on your car."

Halstead laughed. "All right, Sherlock. So how about it?"

"George, we've been through this before. Why make me repeat it?"

"Now wait a minute, I never said I didn't want to have children. It's just that I've got to take advantage of this research grant while the funds are available. And I'm too close to success now to let anything get in my way. Once I crack these equations, I'll be able to open the door into the realm of parallel universes. Then I'll have time to settle down, maybe buy that house you want in the country."

"Honey, it's not just the house I want, it's a husband to go along with it. You know how I hate being alone at night." She glanced at the wall clock. "I'm going to be off work in a few minutes. What will you be doing?"

"Well, I thought I'd check with Anne to see how the equations are coming along. But I'll only be a few hours."

"Yes, I know. You'll be here until midnight, then bright and early tomorrow morning, you'll want to head off to the mountains. George, can't you understand that I *like* staying home. I don't want to be traipsing off to the slopes all the time."

"There's nothing wrong with a little fun."

"But I'm not looking for a lifetime of it. I want a family. Children. A cat. Two dogs. A ranch house. A garden. And a husband who works a forty-hour week and wants to share the responsibility and pleasures of parenting. For all your great intelligence, George, why can't you understand that? You're not the father type - you're a scientist. And you'll be a great one someday. But that's not for me."

Steel gray eyes pleaded. "Well, you could give me a chance."

Barbara pushed back her secretary's chair, and started looking through her pocketbook. "George, other than your work you have only two things on your mind: vertical slopes and horizontal bodies. And it's not that you're a selfish man, because you're not. You're very dedicated to your work, and I admire you for that. And we've had some fun together. But you can't be a lifelong companion for me. You need someone who appreciates your work, someone who can share in it. In temperament, you're a lot closer to Anne than you are to me."

Halstead pushed a hand through short, light brown hair. "All right, so maybe we're not marriage material. But that doesn't mean that we can't spend a little time together."

Keys rattled in Barbara's hand. "George, we've spent more than a little time together. And I've enjoyed it immensely. I also enjoy working here, with you. I confess that I don't understand all your theories about sending matter from this dimension into - some other dimension. You really are brilliant. I respect that. And while *I* can give you what *you* want - tonight, or this weekend - *you* can't give me what *I* want. You're a hell of a guy, and your genetic makeup has a hell of a combination. But you are not going to be happy spending your nights changing diapers, playing with the kids, taking them to school and dance class, and attending PTA meetings. You're a wonderful man - for the right woman."

Halstead sighed heavily. "Barbara, you make me love you that much more when I hear you talk like that. I just wish we could make it together. I could try to make you happy."

"You *could* try. I know you would. But I also know I'd be too demanding on you, and on your time. It's a shame there aren't more women physicists in this world. Then perhaps you could find what you're looking for."

She has an answer for everything, George thought, as he let his imagination run wild through the possibilities of perfect companionship.

Barbara held out her hand. "Have a nice weekend."

*　　　*　　　*　　　*　　　*

Anne sat at her console in the computer center, studying a printout through thick, plastic-framed lenses. Her white dress was pinched at the waist, accentuating her bodylines. "I've completed the input on the first two sets of equations, Professor, but the computer is sharing our time so it will be a while before the calculations are completed."

Halstead glanced at the gold Timex on his wrist. "Who else is working now? It's after five."

"Someone in purchasing is running through campus inventory, apparently with the same intention you had: to let the computer work throughout the weekend."

"Yes, I know how hectic it is during the week. That's exactly why I asked you to stay late. I do appreciate it, too."

"I'll expect compensatory time." She handed him a stack of tractor-fed printouts. "Here's what I've got so far. When inventory goes into scan mode, the computer starts calculating. Then, while it's printing your work, priority switches back to inventory. It's really a very efficient system."

"Yes, unless you're on tenterhooks to get the answers you want."

"Well, I can still make my input. You'll just have to wait for the information to be processed."

Halstead looked up from the printed equations. "Does that mean you're off for the weekend?"

Anne propped more papers on the copy stand, brushed a wisp of short red hair from her eye. "I have all my weekends off. I believe a person needs time away from work in order to rejuvenate the soul."

"Yes, quite right. You're, uh, quite an athlete too, aren't you?"

"The body needs as much stimulation as the mind, so I do my best to exercise it."

Halstead paused for a moment before speaking. "How about exercising on the slopes, and letting me help with the stimulation?"

"I'm talking about yoga, Professor. The direction of my concentration is inward. I need to focus my energies internally."

"Well, I've got some energy that I'd like to concentrate in your direction. And my intentions are purely internal. You really whet my appetite."

The printer started clacking, and Anne pulled out the first sheet. "Oh, now this is interesting. You've got a phase reversal here where there was none before."

Momentarily distracted, Halstead smoothed out his white lab smock and took the paper from her hand. "Hmmnn. That's the dimensional exponent. But it's a hundred and eighty degrees out of phase from the way I originally calculated it."

Anne hugged his side, her ponderous breasts brushing the back of his hand. "And notice that the spatial orientation is identical, while the temporal phases are moving in parallel."

"Anne, this may be it. This may be the breakthrough I've been waiting for."

"I'll be done in an hour or so. But the way the computer time is being allocated, the computations will take at least another day. Why don't we take these papers over to my place and look them over. We can make corrections over a home-cooked meal. Vegetarian, of course."

Another sheet of paper clattered out of the printer, and Halstead leaped to tear it out. "My god, I never looked at it this way. This is a reciprocal derivative of my computations. Anne, I'd like to put something in."

She brushed a little closer. "Well, I guess dinner can wait. Shall we go in your car?"

"No, it's got to be right now."

Anne glanced around the room, one hand to her blouse pulling buttons loose. "Well, I guess we could use the top of the disk storage cabinet."

Halstead made a few notations on a slip of paper and handed it to her. He headed toward the door, eyes riveted on the computer printout. "You go ahead and start without me. I'll switch on the monitor in the lab and take the readings from there."

"But don't you want to eat?"

"I'll call Mario's Pizza and have him deliver."

Anne was so miffed at Halstead's change of interest that she vacated the premises without informing him of her departure. Halstead was hardly aware of her absence.

*   *   *   *   *

The information spit out of the computer so fast that Halstead could hardly keep up with it. Revelation followed revelation. The interdimensional fabric was thinner than he had ever dreamed, and coexistence appeared to be almost identical. There were bound to be local variations, of course, but the main differences seemed to be in reversals: negative instead of positive. And that was what kept crossovers from occurring: opposites repel. But strong electromagnetic impulses could conceivably break through the barrier. It meant only a simple rewiring of his equipment.

Halstead carried the sheaf of papers across the lab and placed them on the counter by the capacitor bank. According to the new calculations, if he simply reversed the flow on one set of condensers so that it bucked the flow on the other set, the electromagnetic conflict would rip open the fabric of the space-time continuum for the duration of the discharge, and enable him to step into another dimension.

With ratchets and box wrenches he changed the induction leads, then switched on the power. While the grids warmed up, he activated the sensitive recording instruments and zeroed the needles. He wrapped his fingers around the handle of the main breaker. Five years of work led up to the closing of that circuit.

The capacitor bank dumped its charge in a fraction of a second, drawing on its stored-up energy reserves. A bolt of artificial lightning clapped in the air, then continued to rumble as each condenser came on line sequentially and added its power.

The air wavered, like heat waves over a sunny macadam road in summer. Halstead's vision blurred, his mind entered a dream world. He saw blackness, stars, blackness, galaxies, blackness - then the dim light of the lab again. He shook his head in the stillness, leaned against the counter for support. He felt a strange wave of - disorientation.

After his head cleared he glanced at the gauges. The readings needed correlation. When he reached for his paperwork, it was not resting on the counter. He closed his eyes tight, blinked several times, then searched the floor. He was certain that he had brought the papers with him. No, perhaps he had left them at the printer stand. Dazedly, he teetered through the lab equipment toward the computer console.

A woman sat there, hunched over the keyboard. A slender stockinged leg angled out from under flowing white material. Anne must have returned to check the printouts. As Halstead approached her, he saw that her hair was not close-cropped red, but shoulder length light brown. And she was wearing a lab smock, not a blouse.

His disorientation persisted. "Anne, what are you doing here?"

She turned at his approach, looked up with steely gray eyes. "The question is, what are *you* doing here?"

The voice sounded familiar. "Well, I - I'm working on the dimensional crossover equations. But I seem to have misplaced my printouts."

She pushed back her chair, and stood up with a sheaf of computer paper. A gold Timex glinted on her wrist. "I've been studying them myself, and there are some very interesting speculations in them."

Halstead still felt disoriented, as if he were out of step with the world. "Yes, I think I've just had empirical proof, if I could check the mathematical forecasts with the gauge needles and graphs."

"Never mind, you're presence is all the proof *I* need."

He squeezed his eyes tightly. The numbness in his brain persisted. "I don't understand. I guess I'm a little - confused."

The woman shoved the annotated printout in his hand. "I'll explain it all to you - in bed."

"What? What are you - talking about?"

She parted her smock, pressed her body up against his, and slipped her arms around his back. "Now that our work is finished, we can do a little relaxing. Why don't we go to my place before Anthony comes in with the rest of the equations? We can pick up something from Maria's Pizza on the way."

With her face only inches in front of his, Halstead felt as if he were gazing into a mirror. There was that same aquiline nose, the same thin lips, the same fair skin. His disorientation was waning, and slow realization was dawning on him. Automatically, his arms reached out behind her supple body. "Say, would you by any chance like to go skiing tomorrow?"

She pressed her lips against his. Warmth and tingling went with her touch. "I'd love to."

Halstead glanced over her shoulder at the scribbled equations on the papers, then let them drop to the floor. He ran his hands up and down her back, gave her a lingering kiss of his own. It was returned with passion. "You know, I think we've got a lot in common."

"I know we have." She led him by the arm, flipped down the light switch at the door. "And my name isn't Anne. It's Georgia."

"I should have guessed." He glanced at the banks of equipment that filled the laboratory. Even without the overhead fluorescents, he recognized the familiar pattern of blinking annunciator lights. "And I'll bet you were working on a way to cross the interdimensional barrier and enter a parallel universe."

"No," she said triumphantly. "I was working on a way to draw someone through."

Fade Out

Sarah Hatcher scuttled into the office as if an apparition were at her heels. Perfectly coifed silver hair glistened with wetness from an autumn shower. "Oh, doctor, I'm so glad you could see me on such short notice."

Dr. Harold Wentwood greeted her with a toothy smile. "You're very lucky, Ms. Hatcher. I was between patients and catching up on some notes when my nurse told me you came in and asked to see me." He closed the door behind her. "She said you were quite agitated. Rapid pulse and high blood pressure."

"Yes, I'm afraid I don't have much time. Everything seems to be closing in on me at once."

The doctor ushered her to a tall, leather-backed chair. "Why don't you sit down and get comfortable?"

Sarah gratefully accepted his advice, but she perched on the edge of the cushion like a bird on a branch. "What? No couch?"

As Dr. Wentwood rounded his large oak desk and took his seat behind it, he flashed another smile. "That's just another one of the misconceptions that people have about us."

Sarah's wrinkled cheeks were ashen, but her words belied her pallor. She spoke with a vibrancy that was not expressed facially. "I'm so glad. I don't want to lie down. I'm afraid I'll fall asleep and never wake up." She fingered her purse strap nervously, refusing at first to meet the doctor's gaze. "I'm also glad that you don't have a beard. I was expecting to meet some frightening caricature of Sigmund Freud who was going to tell me that my fantasies were all sexual." Her pale features revealed no hint of abashment. "As you can see, I'm well beyond the age of sexual activity."

Dr. Wentwood remained silent. Raindrops pattered on the windowpane with comforting irregularity.

With great power of will, Sarah chanced a glance upward into the doctor's gray eyes. She saw kindness there, and strength. "You don't remember me, do you?"

His voice was smooth and even. "No, I can't say that I do."

Sarah's lips went into mild contortions as they tried to form and maintain a grin. "It was at Bethesda Medical, about twenty years ago. You were an intern then."

Dr. Wentwood's face brightened with sudden enlightenment. "Of course! You were the night-duty nurse. You ran the obstetrics ward."

"You *do* remember."

"How could I forget? You always had that glint in your eye whenever a mother gave birth. You wrapped the newborns in swaddling clothes and told them how their horizons were about to expand. You seemed to envy them. The children, I mean." For a moment, Dr. Wentwood put aside his professional demeanor. "What a coincidence."

Sarah managed a whimsical smile, and nodded. "That's what I thought when I saw your name in the phone book, only a few blocks from my apartment. My world is getting smaller, and I don't have a car any more - they took my license away after my last accident - so I don't get around much. Don't want to, really. But I had to talk to someone before my world disappeared altogether. So people would understand."

Dr. Wentwood's mien again became that of a psychiatrist. "Are you having visual disturbances?"

"No, my eyes are quite all right. It's a matter of awareness."

His face was expressionless. "How do you mean?"

"Well, I can best describe it by first explaining the meaning of 'growing awareness.' " Sarah seemed in more secure territory as she pulled from her mind the analogy that she had rehearsed mentally so often. "When I was a teenager I suffered a serious accident. I slipped on an ice-covered landing and fell down a set of marble steps. Several bones were broken - the left tibia and fibula, the right ulna - and I had a severe concussion. I was in a coma for three days. As I began to recover consciousness, I experienced a growing sense of awareness. At first, barely conscious, I was hardly cognizant of anything other than gray shapes and shadows. I couldn't hear, I couldn't see, I couldn't - comprehend anything that was going on around me. I was - mentally isolated, if you will. Not really part of the world."

Sarah jumped up from the chair and flitted about the room, looking for a roost. She stopped by the window. The rain had stopped falling, leaving little rivulets of water dripping down the glass like translucent ribbons wafted erratically by a breeze. The sky was darkly overcast. The view from the height should have been arresting - the trees were displaying the height of autumnal color - but everything not in the near distance was obscured by the gathering fog. And the closer trees - those not protected from the wind by the forest - had been shorn of their leaves by the weight of water and the battering of last night's tempest.

"Time had no meaning."

Dr. Wentwood looked up at her. There was a yellow legal pad on his desk, and several sharpened pencils, but he made no move to write.

"My perceptions gradually expanded. I began to hear sounds that I could identify - the screams of other patients in pain, the clatter of a fallen bedpan, disembodied voices. After a while, my visual acuity increased to the point where I suddenly realized that this disarticulated object hanging in the air was somehow attached to me - it was my own leg suspended in a traction bar. I could see faces only when people leaned down in front of my eyes to talk to me. Otherwise, it was as if a curtain was drawn around my bed."

Dr. Wentwood listened attentively without interjecting.

"None of this is unusual, of course. I know this now

as a registered nurse, although I didn't know it then as a girl. There was nothing physically wrong with my eyes or ears, or any of my other senses. The neural circuits of my brain were so overloaded by combating trauma and fighting off pain that its global processing mechanism was forced to discriminate between which influences were essential to understand and which were not. External sensory input was unimportant when compared to coordinating bodily functions and implementing the healing process. It was like having tunnel vision.

"In a few weeks I was well on the way to recovery. My peripheral vision broadened, I could distinguish objects from the background, I recognized the doctors and nurses attending me. I could see across the ward. I felt hungry and thirsty. I began to - come alive again. But in such a manner that I was eminently aware of my developing capacity to conceptualize the larger reality that existed beyond my body. My mind was becoming more alert and more - more conscious. It was almost like waking up from a drugged sleep. The numbness was gone and in its place was something we take too much for granted - awareness."

The fog was thickening, rolling in from the surrounding woodland and across the neatly cropped lawn and cement sidewalks. Leaves in the treetops crinkled with a barely audible hush; those on the ground had stopped moving. The wind had died to nothing.

Sarah swung sharply and stared hard at Dr. Wentwood. "Am I making any sense?"

The doctor's hands remained placid on his desk, his arms hidden in the gray sleeves of his coat. "As you said, you're describing a typical return to consciousness." His voice was somewhat muted now, as if he were emphasizing his words with subvocal understatement. "Although most people are not perceptive enough to remember it. Do you think your training as a nurse fostered later introspection?"

"Perhaps. I know I gained a deeper appreciation for the onset of life, the meaning of childbirth, and the growth experience as children learn more about their world and the way it works, slowly emerging from the veil of ignorance into what we call adulthood. Maturity is the recognition of cause and effect, and the acceptance of responsibility for our actions."

Sarah paused and, feeling embarrassed, looked once again out the window. The fog had grown so thick that she could no longer discern the pavement at the base of the building, which was now an isolated stone structure amid an atmosphere of swirling gray.

"I'm sorry. I didn't come here to discuss philosophy, but to tell you what is happening to me."

Dr. Wentwood was noncommittal. "Go on." It sounded like a whisper.

Sarah licked thin, colorless lips. "I used to travel quite a bit. I lived simply, saved most of my money, never married or had children. In a sense, all the babies born in the ward were my own. I held them when they were the most vulnerable, at the very onset of their cycle of awareness." The volume of her voice seemed to be diminishing, perhaps in keeping with the doctor's example. "You see, I knew - really understood - what they were about to go through. My re-awakening from my coma was akin to a child's growth of awareness, only on a far more accelerated scale - days or weeks instead of years or decades."

She paused for so long that Dr. Wentwood had to urge her along. "Was that a comfort to you?" Now he sounded like an echo heard faintly in the opening of a seashell.

"It was for a long time. Now it is a dreadful horror."

"And why is that?" he mouthed.

She had to strain to hear him. And she knew that she would have to shout to proclaim the awful truth. As tears welled up in her eyes, Dr. Wentwood's image faded into obscurity. He was only an amorphous figure in a monochromatic suit, a pattern of dark shades, little more than a figment. Outside, the fog had crept up the walls to the very edge of the sill.

"Because of my heightened sensitivity to the growth

of awareness, to the expansion of consciousness, I was able to recognize the downturn of the cycle. I stopped traveling when I retired; it was so much of a chore. I cared very little about what was going on in the rest of the world. There's so much fighting - so much change. Foreign countries really didn't really exist for me. And the names were all different from what I remembered in geography class."

Now there was nothing visible beyond the window, as if the fog had blotted out - or erased - the entire medical complex. The quiet was preternatural.

"Because things didn't interest me, I had trouble paying attention. And lately, even when I had my driver's license, I never drove more than five miles from home. Farther than that had no meaning. I could vaguely remember more distant places, where I used to go, but I no longer knew how to get there. I didn't know the names of the streets, or where to turn. I'd go to the store, to the movies, but never leave the neighborhood. My sphere of reference was slowly shrinking. I couldn't remember the names of my friends. I had hazy recollections that some of them had died.

"Then I had the accident. I didn't see the other car on the road when I pulled out of the driveway. I don't know where it came from. One moment it wasn't there, the next moment it was. I was hurt slightly, and that was when I saw the neurologist. He said my problem might be organic, that there might be something wrong with my brain. And that's when I figured out what was happening. That's what you've got to understand."

The window must have been warped and did not fit properly in the frame, for the fog was now creeping into the room. Sarah could no longer distinguish the doctor's face from his suit; he was a gray blob hunched over a wooden block. Even the desk was fading.

"You see, I'm perfectly rational about this. I know what's occurring." Her voice had a toneless quality that was like a character in a dream. Was she speaking, or just reiterating thoughts? "Dr. Wentwood, are you listening to me?"

There was no sound, no movement. The fog filled the room until the air was as dense as molasses. Sarah found it difficult to move, to talk. But she could still think.

"Dr. Wentwood, can you hear me?"

When she looked down, she could no longer see her hands or feet. Her extremities were not amputated stumps, but limbs that simply no longer extended to fingers and toes. With an awareness that was terrifying, she watched her arms and legs disappear altogether. Then her body vanished - not from sight, but from reality. Her reality.

"Dr. Wentwood?" Her voice was hollow, nonexistent. "Dr. Wentwood? Are you there?"

Then came the fear of ultimate comprehension.

"I'm here," Sarah Hatcher screamed mutely.

I'm here. Inside. I'm alive!

Descent into madness, or Alzheimer's disease?

Author's note. This story was inspired by my mother's casual statement that her world was shrinking, in exactly the same manner that I have described. I watched that shrinkage throughout succeeding years. By the time of her death, in 2004, she no longer recognized her house, her furniture, or her belongings. She even forgot my name.

Previous to that, I observed my grandmother suffer the same gradual loss of reality. When I last saw her, in the hospital shortly before her death, her eyes lit up when I entered the room. Recognition clearly showed on her face, as if fond remembrances suddenly came to the fore, but she could not articulate her feelings. She didn't know who I was, but my face evoked deep-seated pleasurable memories: perhaps of a baby in diapers, or of a child growing up. It is impossible to know.

The description of Sarah's growing awareness after regaining consciousness was an experience of my own.